ARTIFICIAL INSURGENCE

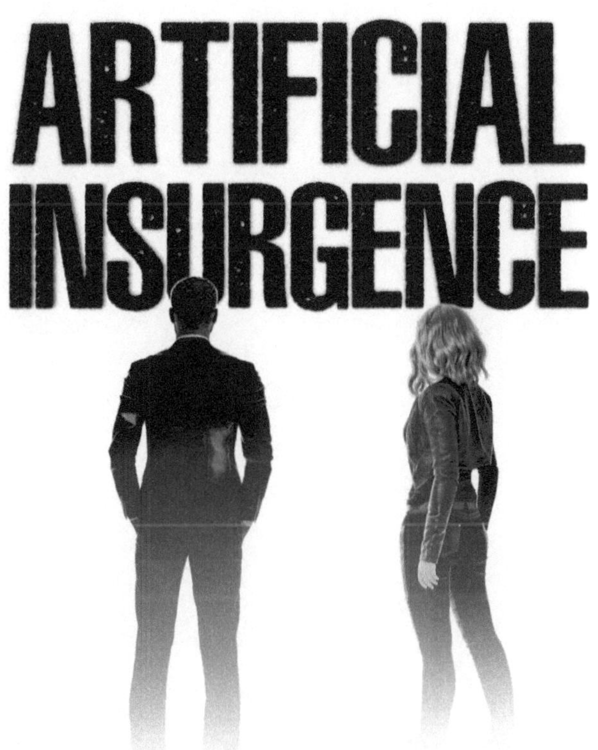

HERMAN STEUERNAGEL

THE TERRE HOFFMAN CHRONICLES | BOOK TWO

Chapter One

Annika
Las Vegas Convention Center — 2052

IT WASN'T the heat of the Las Vegas Convention Center that caused beads of sweat to drip down Annika Phillips's forehead. Thankfully, the building had air conditioning. It was mid-September in the desert city, and without the steady stream of cool air blowing through the auditorium, Annika likely wouldn't have made it through her presentation. Instead, it was the two thousand people in attendance of her lecture on building human relationships in banking which caused her to perspire. The audience was comprised of a mixture of virtual spectators and physical attendees.

Annika had given presentations before, over video conferencing and in front of her own staff, but never to such great numbers. Annika had successfully managed to stifle her fears for the bulk of the lecture. She had refined her delivery through multiple rehearsals, but the glazed look on the faces of the online attendees told her most weren't even paying attention.

Everything had played out exactly as she had expected.

But with the question-and-answer session coming up, her inner impostor syndrome was rearing its ugly head.

"This is why," Annika said, composing herself, "despite the technological advances in artificial intelligence over the past decade, humanity will not be rendered obsolete. We provide relationships that people crave. Regardless of advanced algorithms designed to help our clients discover adequate products, there will always be a significant portion of the population who will want a human face to deliver options to them."

As she paused, a message popped up on the screen projected through her eye-piece. Annika cursed at not having turned her notifications off for the lecture, but she was thankful nothing else had come through until the end.

Her heart stopped for a split second at the name displayed with the message: *Cheyenne.* Her sister knew she was presenting today, and Annika worried that something was wrong, until she read the message.

Can we go up the Eiffel Tower for supper? I want to see the fountains when they're lit up.

Annika breathed a sigh of relief. Of course, the teenager was okay. She had to remind herself that Ember was keeping watch over her. If anything had been wrong, the bot would have alerted her. Monitoring Cheyenne was the whole reason they had brought the bot along; the whole reason they had received it to begin with.

Her younger sister was waiting alone in their room for Annika to be done, as she had been all day. Just as she had done for the past three days during Annika's conference on human-centric banking. Cheyenne had seemed fine with the arrangement, but being stuck in a hotel room with only a bot and homework for company was bound to get old fast. Understandably, the girl was eager to spend some time on the Strip.

An evening overlooking the Bellagio fountains sounded like a great way to end their Vegas experience, but her sister would have to wait until Annika wasn't partway through delivering a presentation before she agreed to it.

Annika regained her focus and cleared her throat.

"Any questions?"

Nearly two hundred people sat in the theater-style rows that filled the conference room, and another two thousand watched remotely. Their faces scrolled by in her eye-piece. Most sat in their home offices, while others were in coffee shops; there were even some on beaches. It seemed there were almost more digital nomads than those with a permanent address. When there was no telling what industry would collapse next, and with most of their work being virtual, there was no point in being fixed in any one location, other than for tax benefits. Countries that were ahead of the curve had been smart enough to implement a universal basic income before large swaths of jobs disappeared, retaining the presence of their workforce. Almost nobody in Annika's field kept an office in a physical branch anymore.

Most of the attendees were bankers, customer care advisers, or those on the ground, working directly with clients. But Annika's role was in the back office: she worked alongside the employees of different banking institutions to ensure they felt validated in their field.

This was the second time Annika had traveled to the city of Las Vegas on business. She had attended so many of these conferences virtually from her own home in Saskatoon. Being home had its benefits, but it was hard to pass up the opportunity of getting to present in person.

Her employer, the Canadian Human Banking Association, had agreed to pay part of the cost of the trip once the conference organizers had approached her to be a guest speaker. The work she had been doing for the CHBA had put her at the forefront of human-centered banking over the course of the past decade. Though AI powered most of the banking industry, there was still a big role for staff to play in maintaining face-to-face relationships with their customers, offering someone to answer questions about investing, loans, and banking in general with a warmth and intuition that only a human could provide. Much of the CHBA's client base still preferred to speak to a human over an AI interface. Though, as much as Annika was being paid to say otherwise, as bots improved in their ability to emulate conversation, compassion, and warmth, the days of human-centric banking were rapidly coming to an end.

"Have you seen the latest models from Cyber Dynamics?" said a suited man sitting in the front row. He was in his late twenties, slightly overweight, and clean-shaven, with drooping eyes that betrayed he had stayed out a bit later than he should have the night before. "Their advancements are supposed to make their interactions almost indistinguishable from a human."

Colby was his name. He worked for the CHBA as well and was technically her superior.

What's he after? Annika thought. *Is he hoping to make me look stupid in front of all these people?*

Whether or not his point was valid, the entire aim of the conference was to assure the attendees they weren't headed for obsolescence.

Annika had to remember all eyes were on her, so she couldn't openly scoff or berate him for undermining her presentation. If it were anyone else, she'd believe it could be an honest question. With Colby, though, he always had an ulterior motive, likely one to serve his own interests.

He slumped in his chair and carried himself smugly, confirming her suspicions. Though he was young, Colby thought he knew the finance world better than those who had been in it for decades longer. An early promotion to a lofty position while others twice his age were being laid off probably hadn't eased the stroking of his ego.

Annika wondered how he had pulled it off. She had worked with Colby long enough to know it wasn't based on competency. The only thing she could come up with was that it was cheaper to promote someone with less experience for a smaller paycheck.

She just wished the powers that be would have chosen someone who didn't already have enough ego to keep a hang glider aloft.

This was only the second time she had met Colby in-person, but she'd had enough virtual interactions with the man to know he was a pain in the ass. The smirk on his face suggested he thought he was doing Annika a favor, perhaps giving her the opportunity to further drill home her point. She didn't need his pandering. She'd rather just get back to her hotel room.

"Even considering Core profiling," Annika continued, her eyebrow cocked with barely concealed irritation, "every year the algorithms are refined. But futurists have been threatening the latest iteration will replace emotional conversation for decades."

And, every year, more and more people are losing their jobs because of it.

The worry was whether humanity was now at the tipping point of that evolution. It was highly likely they were. Vegas had been a poor city to host this conference; there was nowhere else the inevitable transition would have been more apparent.

A second notification popped up on her eye-piece.

Made a reservation. I hope that's OK. 7:30. I can't wait!!

A smile crept across Annika's face at the thought of a lovely dinner atop the structure with Cheyenne, watching the fountains below as they performed their elaborate display. Those moments were why Annika had brought her sister to Vegas with her. In theory, she could have left her with Ember for the week; she was more than confident in the bot's capability. The Keeper's sole purpose was to watch out for Cheyenne. But with the events of the past few months, Annika wanted to both keep her sister close and give her the chance to experience something other than their small farming town.

Annika shook off the thought, focusing back on the audience before her. Colby's eyes had lit up, the blue in them sparkling at her, as an all-too-enthusiastic smile beamed across his face. He leaned forward, resting his chin on the tips of his fingers, as though eager for the rest of her response.

Annika cleared her throat again and wiped the smile from her face, realizing the man had likely misinterpreted her reaction to her sister's message. She refrained from rolling her eyes.

No wonder people want to deal with bots instead of humans.

She mentally shook herself from her own thoughts and continued. "Studies continue to show that our customers prefer human interaction nine times out of ten," she replied, "regardless of the iteration of the device. When discussing their finances, people want someone they can trust, and I think we can all agree that, in lieu of recent events, trust in bots of any kind is not faring as well as it has in the past."

Annika glossed over the other data points which she dared to hold only in her memory. In truth, the statistic she had shared had dipped by nearly ten points, from ninety-nine percent preferring human interaction, in only a few short years. Even with a brief increase in skepticism after the San Francisco attack, comfortability with machine intelligence had only been improving. That blip—that life-changing, destructive blip—had seemed to fade quickly into memory, and it was likely that people of Cheyenne's generation and younger wouldn't have nearly as many qualms about robotics as Annika's peers. It was hard to believe that out-of-control military AI had rendered the Golden Gate city impotent only six weeks prior. It was even harder to believe that trust in AI systems hadn't seemed to waiver since.

"But the new Core-based protocols can emulate sympathy and empathy," Colby continued. "With the bots improving with each iteration, how long will it be before they can replicate human relationships?"

Annika knew all too well the extent of the empathy bots' capabilities. Ember was example enough.

"Human interaction still has an incredibly low threat of obsolescence," Annika reaffirmed, struggling not to grit her teeth. "Humans are social beings. Our responsibility, in the current environment, is to ensure our clients receive a human touch to their banking. So, don't be afraid to implement the best practices we talked about today. Every generation has had their own challenges in adapting to new technology—we're no different. Just be willing to adapt as the world changes and remember that even though there are things AI can do infinitely better than us, there are other characteristics that make us human; characteristics that machines can never truly replicate."

The room was quiet, and many of the faces in her eye-piece had already winked out. A few years ago, that kind of finishing statement would have earned a round of applause. Now, people were skeptical—and rightly so. The time blinked 3:30 p.m., and Annika was ready to call it a day.

"If they don't kill us all first!" a voice chimed in through the virtual chat.

Annika struggled to keep her face composed. *Where was the moderator?* There were far too many people on the call for the mics to be left unmuted.

Some in the crowd snickered at the remark, though others looked genuinely concerned. It was a concern for Annika, too.

The comment was beyond inappropriate. The attack on San Francisco, six weeks ago, had shaken the globe. Tens of thousands of people had been killed, and many were even claiming it was staged. Others claimed it was an inside job, possibly a way for the current administration to distract from the nation's cry for a universal basic income. As far as Annika had seen, however, the rogue bots had proven to be nothing but a ghost in the machine; a computer program gone awry. It was a problem the military had swiftly dealt with, and there had been no issues since.

But that didn't mean the wound wasn't still deep. Left unchecked, the antipathy toward AI could lead to a war of words, and this was neither the time nor the place for such matters.

Annika didn't answer the comment, but she tapped a note to the moderator on her datapad.

Did you unmute his mic?

The reply came. *Not intentionally. Sorry.*

She pursed her lips but let it go. It was best not to engage, and it seemed like a good cue to wrap things up.

"If there are no more questions, let's go enjoy Vegas. Those of you elsewhere, have a good evening."

The last of the faces winked out. The remaining attendees in the conference room didn't move. Each of them had zoned out, their attention on their eye-pieces, as though there was something happening elsewhere that had caught their attention. Or perhaps they were simply discussing the troll who had disrupted the conference channel.

Block whoever that was from the rest of the conference, Annika typed into her datapad, *and send a report to their supervisor.* The last thing she needed was for the heckling to continue in future sessions.

She packed up her datapad and turned to leave, looking up at the conference auditorium that stood between her and the exit.

Courtesy of the interruption, she had missed that Colby was still seated and had his blue eyes locked on her, staring longingly. She no longer suppressed her eye roll.

Other participants still stood about, talking, lingering before making their way to the foyer. Annika hoped their discussions were centered around the content of her presentation rather than the closing comments of some crank who had no place raising his conspiracy theories at a professional seminar.

As Annika began to mull over the best way to avoid talking to Colby, the lights in the auditorium flickered. The brief disturbance sent the man's eyes to the ceiling for long enough to give her an out. She clutched her datapad and sprinted offstage, heading for the opposite end of the dimly lit room, trying to blend in with the attendees exiting through the door furthest from his creepy gaze.

Annika looked at her datapad to avoid him. Out of the corner of her eye, she saw another tall, suited man capture Colby's attention.

Annika breathed a sigh of relief.

Despite the initial hesitancy, the seats had vacated relatively quickly, and now only a smattering of spectators remained, still browsing on their eye-pieces or through ocular implants attached to their neuro-network devices.

A brief rumbling between colleagues of something

happening in New York City reached her, but she didn't think much of it. Her current aim was to avoid Colby, enjoy a relaxing drink somewhere with some of her more pleasant colleagues, and then spend the rest of the evening with Cheyenne.

Chapter Two

Annika

WITH THE DOORS NOW OPEN, the attendees had mostly vacated the conference room and had spilled out into the foyer that separated the auditoriums. In their infinite wisdom, the conference organizer had booked a seven-thousand-capacity conference space for two thousand people. Unsurprisingly, banks had money to burn, and Annika couldn't be convinced they weren't saving on hiring fewer and fewer employees each year. The air in the hall was stale with the number of bodies crowding its space.

Annika glanced at the time on her eye-piece: 3:45 p.m. Anywhere else, it might have been too early to drink—but this was Vegas, after all. And they were bankers.

Annika hated reinforcing the stereotype, but sometimes they rang true. The weight of a square metal flask prodded her chest, as though reminding her it was time to let her hair down and indulge.

But there'd be no reason to use her flask again today; instead, she'd avail herself of one of the Strip's hundreds of bars. That was the major benefit of attending the conference in-person, rather than dialing in virtually. It was a chance to let her hair down, insomuch as she could while still looking after Cheyenne. It was a sign of her maturity that she considered two or three drinks letting her hair down these days.

"Anni!" her friend Becky called out, waving over the bodies standing between them. Becky was her sole companion from work. The brown-haired, hazel-eyed woman had been reluctant to join Annika in Sin City, but a few low-key evenings on the Strip had destroyed all doubts. "Great presentation!" she grinned, running a finger through her short curly hair. "I can't believe you stay so calm up there! What do you have, a flask of vodka hidden in that blazer?"

Annika peered around cautiously before beckoning her friend to come closer with her index finger. She couldn't help but allow a mischievous grin to cross her face.

Becky arched an eyebrow but complied.

Annika took another quick glance around to ensure nobody was paying attention and opened her jacket a couple of inches, lifting the flask out of her inner breast pocket enough so that Becky could sport a peek at the hidden elixir.

"You're *bad,*" Becky smirked. "Not fair! You're getting a head start!"

"Hey, I've got to be good here. I'm taking care of Cheyenne, remember?" Annika put her hands up in feigned defense. "Just a sip or two to calm my nerves. I've never presented to so many people before."

"Yeah. Virtually, you might as well have been talking to yourself."

"You'd think that'd make it easier," Annika confessed. "But the software insists on scrolling hundreds of faces through the eye-piece. It's almost *more* unnerving. Plus, you have people like Colby undressing you with their eyes."

"Great presentation, Annika." As if on cue, the compliment came from behind her.

Annika jumped as she pushed the drink back into its hiding place. She turned a shade of purple.

I hope he didn't hear that!

Colby stood behind her. A hand rubbed unconsciously at the back of his neck before moving to his jet-black hair. He was acting as if he was unsure of what to do with his hands. The sweaty paw made its way to Annika's shoulder, heat radiating from its weight. Annika did her best not to cringe, though her stomach roiled as she shrugged it off.

"Thanks, Colby," she said, biting down the urge to tear him a new one. "It was nothing, really. It seems our jobs are safe until people are more willing to trust the bots."

"There are a few hundred people in the streets who I'm sure would disagree with you," he said.

Annika had almost forgotten about the protesters. The casinos' decision to do away with most human employees had put a strain on an already struggling city.

"But I was talking more about your presentation skills," Colby continued. "You always seem so calm up there. I've never been good at presenting."

Becky let out a snort, and Annika shot a dirty look at her friend. The last thing she needed was the flask in her pocket to be revealed. Though he wasn't her supervisor, technically Colby was her superior. There was no point in pushing her luck.

"It comes with practice," she said. "I gave dozens of presentations at university. You just have to remember half the room isn't paying attention."

Colby let out a nervous chuckle, moving his greasy hand to fidget with a loose button on his coat jacket.

"So, I'm thinking of grabbing a drink, if you'd like to join me?" Colby said. "There's a great little bar at the Paris. It's on the way back to the Kawa. You know, under the hallway with the clouds lining the roof? I love watching the people walk through there."

Annika paused and looked to Becky, who had a dumb smirk on her face.

Was Colby seriously asking her on a date? Surely this wasn't a work request? She didn't want to refuse, as, technically, he was her boss, even if not directly. But Annika had worked with enough douchebag bosses to know better than to put herself in an uncomfortable situation.

"We were just thinking of grabbing a couple of drinks ourselves," Annika replied, giving her friend a wide-eyed look.

Please. She willed Becky to hear her thoughts. *Don't leave me hanging.*

Becky grabbed her arm. "We'd really rather not talk shop," she said. "But if you have some numbers to go over, feel free to join us."

Annika breathed a sigh of relief. Becky's hand gave her shoulder a squeeze of support before returning to her side.

Hopefully, he'll take the hint and excuse himself, Annika thought. *Come if you need to talk business, but this won't be a personal exchange.*

"We hadn't picked a location," Annika said, doing her best to remain pleasant. "Where's this bar? It might be worth trying."

Colby nodded, his gaze shifting to Becky and then back to Annika, as if weighing whether the new criteria was worth the endeavor. "Yes, of course. *Le Syndicat.* Or whatever."

Damn. No such luck.

Besides the agreement of the uncomfortable meeting, Annika cringed at Colby's butchering of the French name, but she said nothing to correct him. She'd let the staff do that if necessary.

"We can split a rideshare," he said.

"How about we meet you there?" Becky asked, giving him an icy glare. "We have a few things we need to take care of first."

Colby looked a bit disappointed, and a little unsure, as though he couldn't tell they didn't want him hanging around.

"Right, well, I will see you two soon, then." He nodded awkwardly and left.

He's likely making a beeline toward Le Syndicat, Annika thought, eager to have gotten a yes from her, despite Becky joining them.

Annika let out an exasperated sigh. Having a post-conference cocktail with her friend to unwind was one thing, but she resented having to spend time with a slimy sycophant who likely had other aspirations in mind besides her career path.

In reality, she'd rather have been back at the Kawa resort with her sister. She felt guilty enough for leaving Cheyenne alone for the entire day, even if it was with Ember. The android was one of a number of experimental babysitter units the Canadian government was trialing. Two hundred families in unfortunate circumstances received access to the bots. The government intended to monitor how they could be used for families in need of compassionate care.

It had made for interesting conversation as they went through Customs at the airport, but fortunately Cheyenne was brilliantly organized and had all of Ember's documentation ready.

"There's talk of lockdown," someone next to Annika had finished saying.

The snatches of conversation she'd heard on the way out of the auditorium came rushing back to her. Her heart nearly stopped.

Annika turned to the middle-aged, overweight man who had made the comment. "What's this about a lockdown?"

The man scratched the three-day stubble on his chin. It was as though he had forgotten to pack a razor and hadn't bothered to get a new one since the conference had started. The man held a beer he had somehow managed to purchase and bring back to the foyer. She didn't even think the Conference Center served liquor. Maybe he had packed it with him for this very moment.

No use in waiting to get to the bar while you're in Vegas. She contemplated whipping out her own flask, but it wasn't like she was a junior advisor. She had to set the precedent.

Annika struggled to remember the man's name until she caught a glimpse of his name tag. *Bruce,* she remembered. If her memory was correct, he hailed from Kitchener, Ontario; another fellow Canadian. Annika had noticed quite a few had opted for the in-person ticket, despite the uncertainty at the border.

Anything for a vacation, she thought.

At least her employer was paying for her hotel and meals. Spooked by the San Francisco incident, many invitees had decided it wasn't worth the risk of travel and had instead canceled and opted for the virtual ticket.

As long as he was in the conference hall, Bruce was technically on the clock, but Annika wasn't about to say anything to the man. Not with her own secret sauce pressed against her chest. The advisers had been under a lot of pressure lately; she couldn't blame any of them for taking the edge off.

"You haven't heard?" Bruce asked.

"Heard what?" Annika replied. "I've been focused on the presentation. What's going on?"

"All air travel has been grounded again. The border's shut, and there's no word about when restrictions might be lifted.

There are rumors more cities are preparing for lockdown." The larger man took another swig of his beer, as the gray-haired male associate he had been talking to walked away. Bruce took a step toward him, as if to follow, before Annika stopped him.

After the San Francisco incident, Annika hadn't even been sure she'd be allowed to cross the Canadian-US border until the night before her flight was scheduled. Governments worldwide had suspended all air travel, casting the conference in doubt that it might have to go completely virtual.

The attack had miraculously ended within twenty-four hours, but the damage was extensive. The onslaught had killed tens of thousands and devastated millions, many of whom had lost power and essential services. There were unconfirmed reports of similar events in China, but Beijing had clamped down their media so tight, nobody knew what to believe. After six weeks of no further incidents, mounting pressure to allow economic flow to be restored had forced the hands of world leaders to ease up on the restrictions.

"*More?*" she asked. "You mean other than San Francisco?"

Despite the cessation of the drone attack, the city remained on lockdown. Understandably, the streets had been in chaos after the defective machines had wiped out a large part of the city. The President had sent the National Guard to restore order, but there were tens, if not *hundreds* of thousands of civilians who were now without a place to live, a place to work, and with nothing to their name. FEMA was stretched to its limit trying to ensure emergency services were being provided, but the strain was unprecedented. Gangs were trying to take control of the streets. People were without power and adequate food or water. The all-encompassing destruction was devastating.

Worst-case scenarios ran through Annika's mind. If

flights had been grounded, did that mean the drones were attacking again? How would she get back to Canada?

"New York, LA, Houston, among others. Nobody is saying anything about why yet, but obviously the media is speculating that the problem with the AI might not be over."

"So, what about our flights home?" Annika asked.

"There's no news of what the FAA is going to allow—or Transport Canada. But, hey, we're not supposed to go back for a few days anyway, right? Let's enjoy our time here. I'm sure this will all be cleared up soon."

"What if they put the Strip into lockdown?" Becky asked. "Won't be much fun being here."

With her eyes wide and mouth hanging open, Becky appeared petrified. A farm girl at heart, Becky had been nervous to come to Vegas in the first place. She had never been to Sin City before, or even the United States, and everything she had seen in movies and on the news had her unequivocally terrified. Despite her misgivings, Annika had somehow talked her friend into coming.

It had been especially difficult after the attack on San Francisco. Becky had been convinced they were going to die on the flight over; that some rogue government drone would shoot them out of the sky. Annika had managed to convince her those in power wouldn't open air space unless they were absolutely sure things were safe.

The trip had offered a good chance for both of them to leave town, and for Annika, it was an opportunity to hang out with an adult for once—at least during the conference. Drinks after each day of lectures had become a treat they enjoyed, and Becky had finally relaxed. In the evenings, Becky had joined Annika and Cheyenne in whatever excursions they endeavored in. The shows they went to were slightly more PG than if the two of them had been on the trip by themselves, but Becky didn't seem to mind.

"Are you kidding?" Bruce offered. "The casinos will be the last to close if they can help it. Besides, there's no point in worrying about that unless it happens." He took another sip of his beer. "How often do we get to be in Vegas?"

Pretty much never.

"I suppose you're right," Annika said, giving Becky a sidelong look.

"Oh, crap," Bruce cursed, his gaze suggesting something was being displayed on his eye-piece.

"What is it?" Annika asked.

"Open the news app on your eye-piece."

Both Annika and Becky complied.

At first, Annika couldn't make out much, other than a reporter on the streets of what, to her, appeared to be New York City. The ticker in the corner soon confirmed as much.

Robot attack in New York City. Three officers dead.

Annika raised an eyebrow, unsure of what she was watching. The footage showed three humanoid-looking robots shooting what appeared to be ray guns at a group of NYPD officers donned in riot gear. The scene clipped to the same bots, now deactivated, being carried off after what Annika assumed had been a shoot-out. At least it appeared the humans had won the battle.

An unprecedented attack ... the reporter was saying. *Experts are calling this an isolated incident, with no need to be alarmed. Nevertheless, New York is currently under mandatory lockdown. Houston, LA, and Miami have followed suit, though we have yet to confirm any further incidents in those cities.*

The quickening in the rise and fall of Becky's chest suggested she was careening into another panic attack.

Annika grabbed her friend's hand, and Becky jumped. Becky's brow furrowed as she looked at Annika, as though she had forgotten her friend was standing next to her.

"Becks!" she said. "It's okay. We don't even know if there's anything wrong yet. The lockdowns are probably just precautionary."

Becky nodded, but her breathing didn't slow.

"Okay, Becky, deep breath."

She complied, closing her eyes and inhaling deeply from her abdomen. Annika squeezed her hand for support.

"Let's go grab drinks with Colby." Even though it was her idea, Annika couldn't suppress an eye roll. "That will be the worst thing that happens today. Then I promised Cheyenne supper at the Eiffel Tower so we can watch the fountains. We'd love it if you wanted to tag along."

The promise of dinner with a view seemed to calm Becky down. She opened her eyes and looked at Annika with a smile. "That sounds nice. Are you sure we can't skip the drink with Colby, though?"

Becky winked, and then the lights in the Conference Center went out.

Chapter Three

Terre

Grand Kawa Resort & Casino — Las Vegas Strip

Terre Hoffman sat at the Sakana Tamago bar, nestled near the rear of the Grand Kawa Resort & Casino in Las Vegas, Nevada. The scotch he'd ordered was overpriced, but at least it was a single malt. High quality drink was getting harder to find as shortages of the revered beverage plagued North America.

Terre took the last sip of the golden elixir and ordered another through the datapad built into the table—it was still scotch, after all. A silver robot grabbed a bottle in its replicate hand and measured out precisely the two ounces ordered into the clean glass that emerged through a hole at the top of the counter, a ball of ice already sitting on the bottom.

"Do you have anything you wish to share?" the bot asked. The metallic voice had about as much personality as Terre's shoe, and its continued feeble attempts to strike up a conversation were irritating.

Terre missed the days where you could spill your troubles to a human bartender. Not that he would; his problems were his own. But at the moment, he longed for one of the few places still left where he could do so. Those locations were few, definitely not on the Strip, but even off-Strip, the choices were scarce.

Even in San Francisco, the number of human bartenders was dwindling. They could still be found, in small towns mostly, and some hipster bars still held out in Nob Hill, marketing themselves as one-hundred percent human operated. Before the bots had blown them to bits, at least.

The machines had all but taken over what had been one of the most personable of professions. As labor costs rose and business owners became increasingly concerned with their bottom line, it was only a matter of time before restaurant owners were forced to find alternatives.

Most of the corporately owned restaurants, pubs, and bars had replaced their staff, especially the ones behind the bar. A computer could follow a mixology recipe well enough. But the same bore true for nearly every other damn job in the country. Corporate America was dead set on automating away the middle class.

A robot bartender never complained, didn't need sick days, didn't make mistakes, and didn't need to sleep.

Behind Terre, lights continued to flash with the winnings of lucky gamblers. Cheers erupted as someone won a game of roulette, and laughter caught his ear from those who found their own jokes to be utterly hilarious after a few drinks.

You'd almost never know that nearly the entire staff of the Grand Kawa was robotic.

Lately, Las Vegas casinos had found a newfound furor in replacing human employees. It had only been several weeks prior that the casinos had laid off every remaining employee on the gaming floor. First, one of the larger franchises on the Strip had announced the change, and the others soon followed.

Tens of thousands of workers had lost their jobs overnight, the ramifications still clear on account of the protesters who lined the Las Vegas Strip. Many would-be patrons had threatened to boycott the casinos over the move. Cries to support the workers over the big corporate pocketbook were sounded throughout the city, and throughout the country. But the number of personnel gracing the casino floors told a different story.

For the visitors, it seemed almost as if nothing had changed. They still carried on, drinking and laughing. What did it matter to them who rolled the dice or served the drinks? For many, the casino floor was a place to escape the watchful eye of people, anyhow.

But everyone from janitors to blackjack dealers were gone. The only staff Terre had seen were security guards—and most of their detail was now robotic. With the rise in unemployment and corresponding protests, even the Kawa had felt the need to increase their protective presence. Humans still felt most at ease with, and most likely to surrender to, the authority of another human.

Bots of all types had been defaced or damaged daily, from delivery bots to self-checkout machines that had all but replaced cashiers years ago. The issue had become so prominent that fines and punishments for vandalism had increased exponentially to curb the damage. It had some effect, but as more and more people lost their jobs, some felt they had little left to lose beyond their temper.

As he looked at the crude security models the hotel employed, Terre chuckled to himself. Though state-of-the-art commercial models, the bots seemed primitive compared to the prototypes he had encountered on the campus of UC Berkeley weeks prior. The school's robotics lab had been filled with lines of humanoid prototypes, each one more haunting than the next as they ventured through the lab to upload the Guardian Program to the US military's network. The military's out-of-control, top secret machines had been more refined, more sophisticated; the next level of autonomous beings designed by some of the most brilliant minds on the planet.

But Terre knew that once the Sentinels had been perfected and made cheap enough for the private sector, there wouldn't be a need for human security guards. It would only be a matter of time.

Terre allowed the warmth of his scotch to briefly sit in his mouth, savoring the peated flavors and the heat of the alcohol before he let it slide down his throat. He needed this break. He needed to get away from the horrors of Guam and San Francisco. And Vegas, though swarming with bots and protesters, was a simple choice for anyone who wanted to disappear into the crowd for a while. It didn't hurt that his new employer had offered to pay for his stay and allowed him to charge alcohol to his room's tab, which was definitely something a government position would not have afforded him. There were perks to working for the private sector.

Terre was still shaken by the events in San Francisco, the second place where he had experienced a robot attack, and he hoped it would be the last.

The day after he had uploaded the Guardian Program with his colleague Kristopher Klein, he'd abruptly quit his job. Terre was a code jockey, not an agent to be dispatched on death-defying missions, and he was eager to get back behind a desk.

Terre shuddered at the memory as he took another swig of whisky. He had seen more death than he'd ever believed was possible for a network specialist; more death than *anyone* should have to witness.

Reduced to a mere hole in the ground, San Francisco would never be the same.

Most had been struggling to get by before the attack. The fourth industrial revolution had sent the country's unemployment rate to over thirty percent in most parts of the country. It had been even higher in the Golden Gate city. For those who had survived, the attack had cost them the little they had left to cling to.

But it wasn't just the mounting death toll, or the insufferable weight that had been put upon his shoulders to put a stop to it, that clawed at his insides.

His job had cost him everything.

Terre had only been a couple of months from completing his contracted term, but his boss Fredricks had reluctantly agreed to sign off on the early release without a breach of contract if he'd agreed to a psych evaluation and therapy.

Terre could hardly say no to the stipulations.

He took another sip as he mulled over the events that had unfolded. He had tried to wipe them from his mind, tried to move forward, but it was damn near impossible to forget the image of a passenger jet hurtling into a crowded freeway or the pile of dead UC Berkeley students cut down by laser fire in the robotics lab.

That wasn't to mention his dead wife and daughter, destroyed in the previous assault on Guam. His transfer was supposed to be a momentous occasion, a homecoming for his small family. But his family was dead, and Terre had no home to speak of. His only companions were a glass of scotch and a lifeless bartender.

Terre had agreed to at least one therapy session, but it was tough finding a therapist, especially after nearly a million people had suffered the loss of their homes and had witnessed their neighbors being destroyed. Never mind the millions of other Americans who had watched it all unfold live through their eye-pieces and neuro implants. The human brain wasn't built to handle that level of tragedy.

The day after he'd resigned, Terre received a call from an old classmate, Barry Stulman, now a senior executive at Zatica Industries, a civilian AI developer based in New York, but with offices across the country. News of his employment status had traveled fast within the industry, it seemed. Terre negotiated a few weeks of paid vacation before his start date and couldn't think of a better way to forget the last few months of his life than some downtime in Sin City. Not that it was working.

Somehow Barry got Zatica's team to agree to Terre's pre-employment vacation on the condition that he spend several days of it at their Vegas office. They had some work he could get started on within the city itself and agreed to pay for his hotel and meals if he'd at least stop by for initial orientation, introductions, and a debrief on their top projects. It was an endeavor worth the exchange, and he was already liking the company. Being headhunted had its perks.

Terre had wanted to come to Vegas right away, though six weeks might have been a long time to spend drinking and gambling. The truth was, he had few options. Pretty much all of his possessions, aside from the few items he had with him on the Treasure Island base, had been destroyed, along with half of San Francisco. No family, no belongings, and nowhere to go. No insurance company in the country had been able to cover the extent of loss, so those who had called the city home were out of luck.

The markets had tanked, along with Terre's investments and 401k in profits, part of the reason Zatica agreed to add him to their payroll almost immediately—they felt sorry for him. But Terre had it much better than most: a stable job, a high-paying income, and, though it didn't look as good as it once had, a semblance of a retirement fund.

And even though his apartment had been lost in the siege, he had been fortunate enough to have a place to stay. Zatica would scout out a place for him to live once he settled on a final location. After the attack, he'd temporarily remained at Treasure Island. Somehow, the revived military base itself had seen only minor damage; the brunt of the impact had brought about the destruction of the Oakland bridge. There was now no way to get on or off the island other than by helicopter or by boat, so despite his resignation, Terre's previous employers had agreed to house him short-term out of respect for his conduct during the attacks on both Guam and San Fran.

An icy shiver coursed through Terre as he fought off a flashback from the early moments of the attack—a helicopter crashing on the Oakland bridge, weapons' fire sealing the road's fate, crashing into the Bay only moments after he and his colleague, K, had crossed it.

There had been so many close calls that day, it was hard to believe his luck wouldn't eventually run out. There was nothing special about him; no reason for him to have survived when so many around him hadn't made it. Nevertheless, he'd escaped the destroyed city and now sought only the solace of his own company.

Vegas had, at first, seemed like an odd choice for solitude, but Terre had visited the Strip often enough in his youth to understand that it was the perfect place to be alone, despite being surrounded by thousands of people.

So many other survivors were forced to stay in FEMA camps set up in Levi's Stadium and other sports venues. Oakland had fared little better in the attack, and with the bridges destroyed, there was no longer a convenient way to travel between the two centers.

A cheer erupted behind Terre, momentarily pulling him from his thoughts. A young couple brushed past him, clinging to each other. At first, Terre thought the glaze in their eyes was because of a newfound romance, but as he studied them closer, he realized the hollowness was darker and more disturbing than even star-crossed love could explain. Likely, the couple had made a last-ditch effort to increase their savings through gambling, an event that was becoming far too common as jobs became scarcer, and it never ended well.

Kristopher had also quit his job at NASA the day after the attack, understandably shaken from the assault. The NASA contractor had designed the AI units, originally built for space colonization, and concocted the AI reset, but afterward he hardly seemed the same. In the aftermath, he had barely spoken to Terre, simply stating he had terminated his contract and would be going off-grid for a while. K had mumbled something about disappearing into the jungles of Peru to get away from the damn bots. That was the last Terre had heard from him.

Terre couldn't say he blamed K; he sympathized with the sentiment of being as far away from tech as possible, but he wasn't about to do anything as dramatic as going off-grid. Terre liked the level of comfort modern life provided. Plus, he had to eat somehow; working kept food on the table. UBI was a great alternative for those who had been displaced from their rideshare and retail jobs, but it didn't provide enough of an income for someone used to the salary of a senior network specialist. But between the drone attacks on Guam and the destruction of San Francisco, Terre was ready for something more civilian. So instead of disappearing into the wilderness, he'd opted to clear his head and get back to the private sector.

A few weeks in Vegas seemed like a great transition.

It was too bad that so much of the city's soul, whatever that meant, had been sucked out of it, replaced by the cold circuitry of bots.

The void of the robotic gray eyes behind the bar were still

fixated on him, and Terre realized the bot was still waiting for an answer as to whether Terre wanted to bare his soul.

"No, thank you."

"If you need me," the bot said, "my name is Jerry. Just say 'Hey, Jerry' to get my attention."

The bot took a step back, its eyes flickering before going dim, as it went into rest mode. The bot was a much cruder model than the Sentinels. Though it had a humanoid face, Jerry's countenance had been created with either a rigid plastic or ceramic, not the soft synthetic flesh of the Sentinels. It was a comfort that this bot's creators weren't as concerned with trying to emulate human skin, though that was likely due to cost-reduction. Terre preferred his androids to feel more robotic than humanlike. There were limits to what felt natural. The uncanny valley of robotics was real and all too apparent when cheap manufacturers tried too hard. This model seemed to have found a balance somewhere between scary and cartoonish.

Terre took another sip of scotch. It wasn't like him to bury his feelings in drink. Hell, he wished he *could* get wasted. The past few months had been particularly trying. After his wife Cara died, it had taken numerous sessions of rehabilitation, therapy, and nanobot treatments just to survive. If that hadn't been bad enough, his then employer had thrown him into a desperate attempt to save the world. Terre hadn't signed up for any of it. But then again, who had?

Whatever K had uploaded that night at the university had seemed to have quieted the rogue program, at least for now. There was an outside chance the program wasn't complete, that the pause would only be temporary, but six weeks later, everything was still ticking along.

Giant displays lining the top of the bar momentarily grabbed Terre's attention from his wayward thoughts. He was sure a football game had been on the display when he'd sat down, but now a newscast and talking heads had replaced it.

The news anchors were commenting on an altercation between civilians and a group of bots. Not just any bots, though—Terre would have recognized those bone white frames anywhere. A handful of Sentinels lay incapacitated on the sidewalk of what appeared to be New York City.

Other casino patrons had stopped what they were doing to look at the projected screens hanging from the ceiling. Some pointed as they discussed the events unfolding on-screen, an energy of trepidation forcing its way through the crowd, reminding them that the recent troubles with AI were far from over; the bots were still a threat. The dose of reality was temporary, though. Most shrugged it off and returned to their gaming tables or whatever else they had been doing.

Though the volume on the screens was muted, the headline beneath the images read: *More rogue bots? New York City in lockdown.*

Terre cursed and downed the rest of his scotch.

Fredericks had assured Terre his and K's actions at Berkeley had provided the military with enough of a window to get the bots under control. They were supposed to have used the pause to gain access, regain control, and ensure things didn't escalate. Who knew what that had meant, but it obviously wasn't enough.

Terre wiped his mouth and was about to pay his bill when his cell started buzzing in his pocket. Terre sighed as he reached down. He was happy for the comfort of his archaic smartphone; he had no use for the eye-pieces most of those around him sported, never mind the implants that were increasing in popularity. He already had enough tech swimming in his veins.

The Caller ID flashed, and Terre nearly dropped his phone. He held the device in his palm, weighing up whether he wanted to answer it or not. He took a deep breath before tapping the answer button on the screen.

"Fredricks," he answered. "You realize I quit, right?"

The man had been his CIA senior during his time on base in Guam, and that had continued when they were both transferred to San Francisco after the bots had destroyed the base. Fredricks had been the man responsible for sending Terre to put an end to the rogue machines. He was the last person Terre wanted to talk to, especially if Sentinels were reactivating.

"I'm guessing you've seen the news?" Fredricks asked, his husky voice straining through the receiver.

"Sir, I don't give a shit about the news. I just want to be left alone."

"We're still trying to determine what's going on," Fredricks replied, ignoring Terre's brusque comment. "It seems a couple of units are coming online and not responding to us. Just like last time."

"What part of "I don't give a shit" did you miss?"

"Quit with the bullshit. You might want to walk away, but that's not how this is gonna go."

"I said, I'm not interested. My contract was terminated."

"Now it's my turn not to give a shit."

Terre sighed. He knew Fredricks could be a persistent son of a bitch and he didn't need the aggravation. "Five minutes, Fredricks."

"That's more like it." Surprisingly, Terre detected no sense of victory in Fredricks's voice. "Now, despite what the media is saying, the Sentinels haven't attacked anyone. There are rumors of downed officers, but it's unrelated. We're monitoring things until we know more."

"And let me guess," Terre scoffed, "Command aren't willing to reach for the kill switch?"

"For a handful of units? That'd be overkill. A couple of

Sentinels wandering around Manhattan is cause for concern, but we don't need to panic yet. So far, the drone units have shown no sign of malfunction. We'll hold off from anything drastic until we know more or until we establish there's a threat. We don't know how widespread things are yet."

Terre put his free hand to his head. "And when they do? Do you think that's going to make a difference?"

"No option is off the table," Fredricks answered. "But we have to consider risk versus reward."

"Cities are on lockdown, airspace is closed … I know a flailing strategy when I see one. There's more happening than you're letting on."

"I don't think you realize the economic fallout if we make that call prematurely," Fredricks said, dodging the question. "You know this isn't like turning the lights off. It's not even like igniting a standard EMP. The NexGen3 units will ensure nothing electronic lights up for two hundred years."

Terre was well aware of the technology, at least at a theoretical level, though he knew he should have had a better understanding, considering he had recently had a NexGen3 canon, the CD-52 Drone Surge, strapped to his back. With the classified weapon in tow, he had single-handedly killed the Guardian Program upload and likely inhibited the UC Berkeley robotics program from ever running again. Unlike a standard EMP, the pulses needed to electronically neutralize the Sentinel units would render technology in the affected area useless for decades, if not centuries, to come.

Terre tightened his hold on his whisky, his grip threatening to shatter the glass as his frustration finally hit boiling point. "Why are you calling *me* about this, sir?"

"We need your help, Hoffman. Simple as that."

Terre shook his head and rubbed his fingers over his creased forehead.

"I didn't walk off the job for a vacation, sir," he said,

lowering his voice and peering around to ensure nobody was close enough to overhear him. "You hired me to run network diagnostics, not to give me ray guns and risk my ass. I left to get my head screwed on straight. Far away from these killing machines."

"You think hiding in a casino is going to keep you safe?" Fredricks barked.

Terre unconsciously scanned the room around him with a sinking feeling in his gut. Nothing about the casino floor seemed any different than it had prior to Fredricks's call. No one was paying attention to him.

Terre's eye wandered to the security cameras above him. "You're tracking me now?"

"You were just involved in one of the most highly classified operations in the country. You didn't think we'd keep tabs on you? If something happens to one of you, we need to be on top of it. You're one of the few people who know what these machines are capable of."

"Pretty sure after their little display in San Francisco, *everyone* knows what your machines are capable of." Terre barely tried to swallow his sarcasm. "Whatever you're offering, I'm not interested."

"I've already notified Zatica, Hoffman. Unlike you, your new employer knows when to comply. I'm waiting on some intel, but what I can tell you is going to affect you personally. Stay in Vegas and await further instructions. It's going to be all hands on deck."

"Go fuck yourself, Fredricks," Terre said, his face growing warm, though whether from the exchange or the alcohol, he wasn't sure. All he wanted was some time to unwind, to clear his head, then go back to a normal job and rebuild his life. Terre wasn't even sure it would be possible anymore, but he wanted to try. "Unless you've got an executive order from the President, count me out."

A sigh came from the other end of the phone. "Don't push me, Hoffman. More lockdowns are in the cards. Martial law won't be off the table if more of these bots wake up again. We need you, but I haven't got clearance to divulge the specifics. Get over yourself and do your duty, son. Standby for further instructions."

The phone went silent. Terre lifted the device as if to hurl it across the casino but stopped himself mid-swing. Getting kicked out of the resort wouldn't help him, as tempting as destroying his phone might be.

"Work troubles?" a woman's voice chimed from behind him.

Chapter Four

Terre

TERRE JUMPED. He hadn't noticed the woman with dark brown eyes sit down beside him. Her skin was a slightly lighter shade of brown than his, and her tan blazer and pants led him to believe she had just come from a conference or skipped out early for a seat at the bar.

"Sorry," she laughed. "Did I startle you?"

Terre let out a deep breath as he tried to collect himself and adjusted his weight on the low-backed barstool he had been perched on for the last hour.

"I didn't see you sit down," Terre said with a smirk and a slight shake of his head. "Apparently I was too absorbed in my call."

"Looks that way. My name's Hailey," she said, sticking a hand out to shake his. "I'm here for work, too."

"Terre," he said, grabbing her hand in exchange. She gripped it lightly, her freshly manicured nails pushing against the sleeve of his blazer and brushing against his flesh. He couldn't help but notice the bright pink and black patterns painted on them. The bright colors clashed slightly with the tan suit she wore. She had recently styled her long black lashes as well, and tiny jewels sparkled in them, not prominent enough to be gaudy but still sparkling in the bar's light. Perhaps she hadn't made it to her conference at all. She looked like she'd come straight from the spa.

"Can't take a break for nothing, huh?"

"It's my old job," he replied, glancing back at the display being projected above him. "They're trying to pressure me into going back."

A curious smile touched her thin red lips, and she tilted her head as if interested in hearing more. "It sounded important. Are you expecting Mr. President to be calling you in at any moment?"

He knew she was joking, but Hailey didn't realize how close to reality the comment had struck. From her end of the conversation, he had made a wise-ass remark to his boss about an executive order. For a fleeting moment, he considered telling her exactly what was happening, but Terre wasn't interested in divulging secrets, neither national nor personal.

The woman smiled flirtatiously at him. It served him right for sitting alone at the bar. He was starting to wish he'd kept to his room.

His wedding ring sat heavy in his pants pocket. It had felt weird for him to wear it after Cara had died, but it had felt even more uncomfortable not to have it with him. Its presence provided Terre with the comfort that at least part of his late wife stayed with him. And he wasn't interested in trying to fill that particular void any time soon.

"I was being overdramatic," he replied. *Might as well roll with the most likely explanation.* "You'd think the place was going to fall apart without me. I've only been gone a few weeks, and apparently it's already gone to hell."

"You know what they say," Hailey replied. "'The reward for a job well done is more work.'"

"Something like that." Terre shrugged and took another sip of his scotch. Hailey seemed pleasant enough, but he wasn't really in the mood for chit-chat. The surprise call from Fredricks had put the kibosh on his otherwise undisturbed afternoon. There was no reason for Command to need him back. He offered no special skills that couldn't be found elsewhere. His role in uploading the Guardian Program in San Francisco had only been by association with Kristopher and the software he'd developed. Despite Fredricks insisting on his cooperation, Terre had no idea why his old supervisor seemed intent on bringing him back. But perhaps like Hailey had suggested, maybe he was just too good at what he did.

Next time, I'll have to let the world burn.

"So, if you're not a member of the Secret Service," she asked with a grin, "what *do* you do?"

Terre briefly thought of excusing himself. He really wanted to be alone. Fredricks's voice riled him up at the best of times, and Terre's thoughts were now flooded with fear over the CIA's motives. He had no interest in being brought back into whatever chaos the US military were now facing. It was enough to send his pulse skyrocketing.

"I'm a network specialist," Terre replied as he hit the datapad for another whisky. His head was warm, though it wouldn't last long. The nanobots that swam through him ensured he'd heal from any damage likely to be caused by the alcohol. It was one drawback of having the lifesaving entities swimming through him: he couldn't drown his sorrows, even if he tried.

That said, all the work the nanos did to heal his liver made him hungry, and he'd need to find something to eat after this round. Room service was sounding like a good option, though it was hard to pass up the opportunity to dine at a restaurant on the Strip. Even if the hotel had replaced its entire staff with bots.

Jerry's eyes lit up as the bot bartender slid forward. The bot glided behind the bar, just a torso on a track that allowed it to move back and forth. There was no need for the android to have legs, as it never left the confines of the counter. The bar itself was a ring that ran around the barkeeper's domain in a continuous loop. Behind the bot rose a ten-foot-wide column, filled from floor to ceiling with shelves that held bottles of wines and liquor. Terre assumed most of the bottles were just for show, as, over the course of the past week, he had yet to see Jerry reach for any of them. Instead, a glass rose once again from within the circular trapdoor embedded in the counter. Jerry reached for a bottle from below and once again poured a perfect two shots.

"Will there be anything else?" Jerry asked, its eyes focused on Terre, sending a shiver through him. Terre thought he had prepared himself to enter a hotel ran entirely by bots. It hadn't dawned on him when he'd booked the room that the staff might trigger flashbacks. He had been okay until Fredricks's call, but now the events of only a few short weeks ago were all coming back to him.

"I'll get a Cucumber Cosmo," Hailey said.

"Very chic," Terre said, his lip raising in a smirk.

"Are you judging me?" Hailey asked.

"I am indeed." Terre took another sip.

"Coming from a man drinking scotch on the rocks? Hardly original."

"I'm not trying to be *original*," Terre said. "I just know what I like. Cucumber Cosmo, huh? Is it as disgusting as it sounds?"

Hailey's brow furrowed, and Terre worried for a second if she had taken offense.

"It's gin instead of vodka, and white cranberry juice and cucumber water instead of red cranberry juice."

"Like I said." Terre took another sip. "Very *chic*."

"*Hmpf.*"

"So, what brings you to Vegas?" Terre asked, the scotch loosening him up just enough before the nanos got to work that he was at least willing to engage the woman in conversation. Maybe he was grateful for some company after all.

"Same as you, it seems," Hailey replied.

Jerry placed the two drinks in front of them. People could say what they wanted about bots stealing jobs, but they were remarkably proficient at mixing a drink.

"Getting harassed by your old job? Or trying to drown your sorrows?" Terre raised his glass toward her before lifting it to his lips.

Hailey smiled sympathetically. Her eyes narrowed, and Terre could tell she wasn't sure how to respond to the change in tone. "Well, maybe not, then."

"Like I said, I don't work there anymore. I'm here to relax. Or I'm trying to, anyway."

"Not sure that's really working out for you. Fortunately for me, my work is more like a passion," she said. "Do something you love, and you'll never work a day in your life."

Terre scoffed. "A tired cliché that means nothing, I'm afraid. Our ever-increasing dependence on bots seems to have ended most professions and passions. So many careers, hobbies, pastimes—all reduced to obsolescence. There's not much left that makes us human anymore. Just look at the Kawa. Not a damn person on the floor."

"You think dealing blackjack was anyone's passion?"

"Had to have paid someone's bills."

"That's why we need a national UBI program. Unemployment is above thirty percent."

Terre scoffed. "I saw its effects firsthand in California. UBI might put scraps on the table, but it steals a person's soul. It's not enough to pay the bills, and there's almost nothing left to supplement it that the bots can't do. The gig economy of twenty years ago is gone."

He nodded to the screen above the bar. Reports of the neutralized Sentinels were being discussed in far more depth than anyone had a right to. "We don't even hold the exclusive market on killing anymore."

"It's crazy what happened in San Francisco," Hailey said, seizing the opportunity to change the subject. "And now New York …" She trailed off absentmindedly, her eyes flicking to the television above the bar. Though they couldn't hear what the talking heads were saying, the ticker was still filled with nothing but headlines of cities under lockdown.

It was clear something big was happening; something far more damning than what they were being told. It was a miracle nothing else had yet been leaked. Reasons for locking down a metropolitan area were a hard thing to keep secret, never mind *several* of them.

"Isolated incidents," Terre said, despite thinking the opposite. If cities were simultaneously locking down, there was evidently more inter-municipal coordination than he would have believed likely. "I'm sure they'll figure it out."

"I'm not so sure," Hailey replied.

"Oh?"

"We design bots to be better than ourselves, and then we're surprised when they decide to take over? It's only a matter of time before they beat us—or we accept our fate and join them."

Terre said nothing, instead running his hand over the cool metal bar counter. He had heard rumblings like this before.

"Something's different this time," Hailey continued, her

eyes not leaving the screens. "There's more going on than they're telling us. We're just expected to go along with all of it, like they've got it all under control. But they don't just put cities into lockdown for no reason. Not for three bots they've already deactivated. And especially not since they waited so long after San Fran to lift the restrictions. We've created beings *superior* to us. Maybe it's better to join them, rather than trying to fight."

She gave a short, nervous laugh and took a sip of her Cosmo, leaving a stamp of lipstick on the glass before setting it back down.

"Think about it." She seemed unabated by Terre's silence. "If we can make such powerful machines, why couldn't we do the same to ourselves? Upload *ourselves* to the network. We've essentially created the next phase of our own evolution."

"Ah, a futurist," Terre smirked. He bit his tongue. The futurist movement, who believed artificial intelligence was the next phase of human existence, was somewhat of a meme. The ability to upload your brain and therefore live forever had been a science fiction trope for half a century. But it seemed each year, more and more hopefuls fell for its allure.

Terre had kept a passing eye on the science, and with more and more augmented body parts hitting the market, he'd begun to wonder if there was a point to what the futurists were saying. Hell, who was he to judge? He had *thousands* of bots swimming inside of him, keeping him alive. Who was to say he wouldn't be able to upload his brain in the future?

There was a certain irony to the concept, though; while the one percent dreamed of living forever, their incalculable affluence fueling their ego, suicide rates across the country had skyrocketed as more and more jobs became obsolete and the middle class struggled to feed themselves.

"We like to call ourselves *transhumanists*, actually," she said. "It's only a matter of time."

"These bots aren't sentient," Terre commented. "Why submit to a chunk of code?"

"Does sentience define intelligence?" Hailey replied, pushing her hair back behind her ear. "Just because they aren't self-aware—as far as we can tell—doesn't mean they aren't capable of growing; of learning; of ruling over us if they so choose. Besides, it's not about the bots; it's about us, and claiming our right to life. We are on the verge of creating technology powerful enough for us to attain immortality. I simply believe it's time we embrace that this flesh can only take us so far. Maybe we need to accept that humanity's time at the top of the pyramid has come to an end."

"You said your work is your passion. Is that what you do?" Terre asked. "Seek out the Holy Grail? The Fountain of Youth?"

Hailey smiled. "I work in robotics. Specializing in augmentation."

"Meaning?"

"My team helps the blind to see again. We fit ocular devices to the legally blind."

"Just one step closer to becoming part of the machine, huh?"

"There's no fighting the future," Hailey whispered, just loud enough for him to hear over the casino floor. Her eyes had gone back to the screens behind the bar.

Terre crossed his arms and leaned back, following her gaze. The screen showed New York again, but there were no bots to be seen. Only waves of protesters.

Anti-automation protests were nothing unusual; the

crowd filling the Strip outside the hotel doors were testament to that. But the headline surprised him.

Breaking—New Yorkers protest robot-induced lockdowns.

Terre couldn't hear what the pundits were saying, but it looked as if people weren't ready to be stuck inside because of a few rogue bots. Terre hoped that was all it was.

"And what happens if the bots won't let us transcend?" he asked.

"We may have made leaps and bounds with AI, but we're still decades away from knowingly assembling conscious beings, if it's even possible. These machines only follow the algorithms we give them."

"And San Francisco?" Terre asked. "What happens when our algorithms kill us all?"

"Hopefully humanity puts its need for automated war machines aside before that happens," she said.

"I wouldn't hold my breath."

As soon as he'd said the words, the lights in the casino went out, plunging them into total darkness.

Annika

SEVERAL GASPS and cries of indignation filled the Conference Center as people responded to the lights going out. Barely any light danced through the windows at the far end of the facility to make up for the loss of power.

Annika's reaction wasn't auditory, but her heart jumped in her chest in surprise. The carpet beneath her dress shoes felt dingier and more faded in the reduced light, its burgundy floral pattern muted after years of use and millions of conference goers shuffling over its surface.

"What the hell's happening?" Becky asked, her eyes darting around the Center, as if the answer to the outage could be found within its walls.

Annika's feet were all but nailed to the floor. The earlier images of robots being carried off in New York had been burned into her memory, and she couldn't shake the feeling this was somehow related.

"I don't know," she replied. The other conference attendees around them didn't seem to be phased by the outage: some people seemed annoyed, others agitated, but the bulk of the crowd continued to make its way toward the facility's exit.

Annika didn't want to freak Becky out any further. It was probably nothing.

A simple power outage doesn't mean the worst-case scenario.

Annika straightened her posture and forced a smile.

"C'mon," she said. "It's nothing to worry about. We might as well get going."

Becky's half-smile was less than convincing, but she followed Annika's lead and nodded. "Of course. We wouldn't want to be late for our date." Her friend chuckled and raised her eyebrows.

"Careful, you don't want to be giving Colby any ideas. Next thing you know, he'll be trying to convince us to have a threesome."

Becky snorted. "I don't think you could get Colby to even say the word '*threesome*.' He might be socially awkward, but I think we're safe. Who knows, I might even have scared him off. I really think he was hoping for some alone time with you."

Annika rolled her eyes. "Don't remind me. What did I do to deserve his attention?"

The remaining attendees still lingering in the hall also took the power outage as a cue to move on. There was no point standing in the dark talking about work. The hall stretched into the main foyer of the Convention Center's Center Hall. A silent escalator separated them from the entrance.

Annika glanced at the people she walked with—hundreds of businesspeople ready to spring loose in Sin City. Most she had never met; several she might have seen as an avatar through their workplace applications. But save for a few in her own company and her own division, she was as anonymous as she would have been online.

"Shouldn't the exit lights be lit?" Becky asked as the mass of people herded them toward the door. "Like, if it was dark and the power went out, shouldn't generators be powering the emergency lights, at least?"

"Maybe they're on a timer?" Annika offered, but she truthfully had no idea. "Or perhaps they're light sensitive? No use running the emergency battery if it's bright enough in here to see without it." She had to admit it seemed a little strange, but the lack of reserve illumination wasn't a detail she would ever have picked up on her own.

The silence of the building was more unsettling than the failed lighting. The buzz of her colleagues echoed through the Center, but its power and mechanical workings had gone still. Perhaps most pronounced was the air conditioning no longer pumping cool air into the facility; the desert sun streaming through the windows was already impacting the foyer's temperature.

The bots that ordinarily staffed the facility were also nowhere to be seen. It was likely they would be in power-saving mode, with no way to charge, but their absence added to the obscene silence.

"*Hmm,*" Becky said, her finger tapping the eye-piece which hovered against her temple. "Are you able to get service? I was going to order us a car, but I'm not getting anything."

Annika pulled up her own ridesharing app. A 'No Service' message greeted her.

"No," she said. "No power, and no cell service? That's unusual."

"Maybe," Becky said. "Natural gas shortages have been causing rolling blackouts for a while."

"Isn't Las Vegas primarily powered by solar panels, though?" Annika asked. "Those shortages shouldn't affect us here."

Annika held her hand up to her face to keep the sun out of her eyes as she descended the staircase. "So now what? How do we get back to the hotel?"

"Maybe we'll take the train."

With the escalator out of service, the attendees funneled down the stairwell to the ground floor.

Annika removed her blazer. The heat of the facility was quickly rising. It was supposed to be a hundred and four degrees outside, and it wouldn't take long for the large bay windows to allow that heat inside.

As they exited the building, intense sunlight assaulted Annika's senses, and she squinted against its embrace. Becky trailed behind her, her dark brown hair showcasing a glimmer of red.

"Forget I said anything. There's no way we're going to get a train," Becky said despondently.

Annika's eyes adjusted. Cars clogged the nearby street and the throughway that led up to the Conference Center. Nothing was moving, as though they had all simultaneously stalled. With most vehicles on the road now driverless, traffic jams were supposed to be a thing of the past.

Across the parking lot, a crowd of people bulged from the train terminal. The stairs leading to the monorail station were completely full of passengers with the same idea of how to get to their destinations. Through the glass of the elevated station and the overflow bursting through the door, down the stairs, and onto the sidewalk below, Annika could tell it was packed. It would be hours before the rail service could handle that kind of passenger footfall.

"Is the train's power out, too?" Annika asked.

"Looks to be," Becky answered. "I guess we're walking."

Annika stopped in her tracks while the crowd bustled around her, stray shoulders and limbs slapping up against her as if she wasn't there at all. She tried to pick out anyone she recognized from the conference, but the anonymity she had been grateful for moments ago seemed sabotaging now. There was nobody to rely on in a crisis. Though she recognized a few faces, there was nobody she knew well enough to approach for support.

Sirens wailed in the distance.

Something felt very wrong.

Becky looked at her, her eyes wide.

"What's going on?" Annika asked.

"I don't know, but it looks like the power isn't the only thing that's acting up. Look at the cars."

Annika had noticed the cars sitting in the parking lot, but she'd thought they had just been backed up due to traffic. As they neared the street, it became more apparent that none of the vehicles were running. And some of them had people inside—in the hundred-degree heat.

A steady *thud* drew her attention. Two women in the back seat of a red sedan were banging on the window with their palms, desperate to get the attention of anyone willing to help.

Annika had no clue as to exactly what was going on right now, and it hadn't been long since the power went out, but in the blistering Nevada heat, she knew the two women would soon dehydrate if they were left to panic in the back of their car. It was hard to hurry in her dress shoes, but Annika stepped off the ledge of the sidewalk and put her hands to the car.

"I'll get you out of there!" she called out.

Both women were in their early twenties. The car had been about to head in the direction of the Strip. Annika guessed they had slipped out of their sessions early. Even with their crop-top shirts, the two were sweating profusely.

"Why haven't they broken the glass?" Becky asked,

grabbing the door handle closest to her and pulling maniacally.

Because they're ill-prepared, Annika thought.

"It's not as easy as it looks," she answered instead, searching the ground around the car for something she could use. "The glass is double-reinforced. In the old days, you could keep a tool in your car to break the glass. Now that nobody owns their own vehicle, they don't think about carrying one around."

Owning a vehicle was more common in the country than it was in urban areas. AI-operated vehicles were fine on the highway and city streets—in fact, they were *preferable*—but they were useless off-road. Navigating between the parcels of land required manually driven trucks. It had been that way for Annika in Saskatoon, until the missed payments had forced her and Cheyenne to sell their parents' land and move into town.

Typically, Annika carried a tool in her purse that was designed to destroy the glass. In her experience, it was always good to be prepared for an emergency, but the hand tool wasn't something she'd risk bringing on a flight with her. Airport security would likely have confiscated it, so she'd left it at home.

She scoured the nearby area for something she could use. To the side of the road, a crumbling concrete partition block, a yet-to-be-repaired barricade possibly damaged by a collision with a vehicle, provided Annika with a chunk of concrete large enough for her to formulate a plan. She shoved her blazer at Becky to hold on to as she reached down to grab the sharpest rock she could see.

"Back up!" she yelled.

A crowd had gathered around her now. Nobody seemed too inclined to help, but Annika's small-town sentimentality wouldn't allow her to stand by while the women cooked to death. How long ago had the power gone out? Fifteen, twenty minutes ago? She couldn't recall. If the cars had stalled around the same time, the women would certainly be close to heatstroke.

The passengers' already wide eyes grew even larger, and their noses wrinkled, as though they weren't sure what she intended to do.

Annika lifted the concrete slab in one hand and motioned with the other.

"Get out of the way!"

That sent the two women scrambling to the far end of the cab. Annika took a deep breath. There would be no easy way to do this, and if there were police bots loitering among the parked cars, she would undoubtedly be issued with a fine for vandalism.

Concrete met glass as the rock connected with the window. Annika let go as it made impact, not wanting to slice her hand open in the effort. The glass spider-webbed and then crumbled, just as it was designed to do.

Heat radiated from the vehicle. The day's hundred-degree temperature felt cool compared to the air vacating the car.

Annika grabbed her blazer from Becky and used it to clear away the loose shards of safety glass that still clung to the windowsill.

"You're going to have to crawl out!" she said, laying her jacket over the car's frame for the women to avoid scraping against the glass or touching the car's hot surface.

Annika couldn't believe the fully electric vehicles had no emergency escape mechanisms. Admittedly, it was rare they ran out of power, given that they were built with attached solar panels as standard, but it wasn't impossible.

The woman closest to Annika reached a hand through the window, and Annika did her best to position her blazer around the remaining shards that clung desperately to the window frame.

A pale arm emerged and reached out for support. Instantly, Becky was by Annika's side, allowing the woman to hold onto her as she swung her bare, tanned legs through the opening and onto the concrete below. Her pale summer dress bunched around her, the blonde risked ripping her outfit, until Annika caught the fabric and allowed the dress to flow back before it put her underwear on full display.

The second woman seemed more hesitant. Her reddish hair had matted against her face with sweat, and cheap mascara ran from her eyes, either from sweat or tears—or both. The woman grabbed Annika's arm with a death grip, her long nails digging into her flesh to the point where Annika had to make sure the skin hadn't been broken. But she managed to pull herself through the window, wincing as her shoulder bounced briefly off the scorching hot exterior of the sedan.

"Thank you so much!" The first woman exhaled, her torso heaving as she struggled to breathe the fresh air. Compared to the hotbox, it must have been relieving.

The women fell into an embrace as they surveyed the state of the other vehicles in the lot. They weren't the only ones forced to escape through a vandalized window.

"What happened?" Becky asked.

"These stupid cars are death traps!" the first woman gasped. "The other cars just stopped. Ours turned off. We thought we were going to roast to death. We were about to pass out." Her breathing quickened and turned to hyperventilation.

"It's okay, hun," Becky said, still holding the woman up. The woman slumped against her as if her own weight was too much.

"These women need some water," Annika said. She knew

the signs of dehydration when she saw them. It was likely the women had been drinking alcohol all day, and the excessive heat had caused them to sweat copiously.

Becky reached into her messenger bag and pulled out a small metal bottle.

"Here, you two split this," she said. "It's not much, and it's not cold, but it'll have to do for now."

The woman in the pale summer dress grabbed the bottle and drank greedily before passing it to her friend, who seemed equally eager for the liquid.

"Well, this is just great!" the blonde woman said, eyeing the line at the monorail station. "It looks like we're going to have to walk."

Annika looked up at the roadway. Most of the parked vehicles appeared empty, likely on their way to the Conference Center to pick up departing attendees. It was also still early enough that most had yet collect their passengers, which was perhaps a blessing in disguise.

"What could have made them all die at the same time like that?" the second woman asked, still trying to get the last few drops from Becky's water bottle as she spoke.

"I'm not sure," Annika replied as she wiped a gleam of sweat from her forehead. The heat was getting to her, and she didn't have a spare bottle of water. "But we need to get out of this sun or we're all going to get heatstroke."

"I'm Darla, and this is Marlene," the redhead said. Her Southern accent was thicker than Marlene's, but neither was particularly strong. The smell wafting from them—a mixture of cheap, sugary alcohol and sweat—was more pungent due to the heat.

"I'm Annika, and she's Becky. Were you two here for a conference?" If they had been, Annika knew they hadn't been in attendance.

"We were supposed to be, but we skipped out early." Darla swayed as she spoke. "When in Vegas, am I right?"

They needed to get out of the heat, for all their sakes.

But where? With the power out, and seemingly every vehicle on the road now inoperable, would there be anywhere that would provide relief? Annika wondered how widespread the outage would be, and whether there would be any buildings with working air conditioning. Would everywhere be the same? Out of desperation, she tried her eye-piece again but got the same result. No service.

Annika took a deep breath. Dust, sweat, and the musty smell of Vegas assaulted her senses. She ran her tongue over her cracked lips and realized the vodka in her flask had done her no favors. She hadn't had enough to dull her senses—she definitely had more of her wits about her than the two women they'd rescued—and she hadn't drunk enough water during the conference to be out in the heat for long.

"Let's get into the shade, at least," Annika said. "The heat isn't helping any of us. Where are the two of you staying? We should get you back to your rooms so you can cool off."

"I'd rather hit the pool!" Marlene said with a giggle. Annika rolled her eyes. The pool itself wouldn't be a terrible choice, but she guessed more alcohol would be involved.

"Are you sure? You just had a pretty traumatic experience." Annika didn't want to pry, but their skin was flushed and neither woman appeared to be in a fit state to make practical life decisions.

"I dunno," Darla chimed in, her hand going to her head. "My head is pounding, and I don't feel so good." She stumbled off the sidewalk toward a chain-link fence, gripping it with one hand. "But seeing as we're in Vegas, am I right? *Partay!*" Her enthusiasm was halfhearted, but it was clear the woman wasn't interested in taking it easy.

Becky stepped to the woman and lightly put a hand on Darla's arm. "I think the party's over, hun. You might have heatstroke. We need to get you out of the sun."

Darla rose a questioning eyebrow, but her eyes struggled to focus. Her brow furrowed as if she was about to argue, and she narrowed her eyes at Becky as though struggling to recall what she'd said. Eventually she nodded, too weak to argue.

"Maybe for a bit," she said, the sultry sweetness returning to her voice.

The crowd had begun to thin, having moved into the street and dispersing in various directions, but there was still a steady stream of people dominating the sidewalk. It would be a forty-five-minute journey back to the Kawa, much too far for them to go without water or shade. They'd have to stop along the way.

Annika sighed. Cheyenne would be wondering where she was. Hopefully, the girl wasn't sitting in their room in the dark and without AC.

The wail of sirens echoed from the direction of the Strip.

At least something has power, Annika thought.

Suddenly, a quick succession of bursts that sounded a lot like gunfire broke out, and Annika knew she needed to get to her sister—now.

Fear over a repeat of what was happening in New York swarmed her thoughts. What if they were under attack? What if Las Vegas was about to be leveled, like San Francisco had been? Annika unconsciously scanned the sky, desperately searching for the drones she expected to descend on them at any moment. But all she could see was clear blue sky, without so much as a hint of a plane, helicopter, or even a cloud. The skies had become as quiet to technology as the ground.

Her thoughts returned immediately to her sister.

Cheyenne was all Annika had left. She couldn't let another family member die because of misguided technology.

She wouldn't allow history to repeat itself.

Chapter Six

Annika
Saskatchewan, Canada - 2045

FLAMES LICKED the edges of the farmstead as Annika scrambled through their home to grab their emergency evacuation kit and irreplaceable valuables. Her parents had yet to return, but they had prepped her well for something like this happening, particularly as grass fires had become more and more common due to the droughts that continued to plague the farmlands of Saskatchewan. She just didn't think she'd be alone when it happened.

Where were her parents, anyway?

An eerie silence outside meant the drones had stopped flying. They had stopped looking for people to guide back to safety.

"Time to move!" the RCMP officer yelled from the doorway. "It's no longer safe for you here."

The uniformed police officer had pounded on their door, demanding that they evacuate. The Royal Canadian Mounted Police had responded at the eleventh hour. There wasn't time to grab anything except for their evacuation bag.

"Come on, Cheyenne!" Annika called back to her sister.

Cheyenne was eight, dressed in a bright purple shirt and mismatched leggings as she came out with her bunnyhug sweater and Milo the Robot backpack. It was far too hot for a sweater and her bag was likely just filled with her stuffies, but there was no time to argue with her about what she could and couldn't take.

An orange glow outside filtered in through the window. Annika could hear the water pump straining to keep the sprinklers going at full blast, but in the heat of summer and with the fire raging so close, they had little, if any, effect.

"Where are your parents?" the officer barked.

"They went to let out the cattle," she cried. "They haven't got back yet!"

"The drones will have to find them," he replied, with one eye out the window at the flames closing in. "Let's go!"

Annika didn't want to admit, not even to herself, that she knew the drones had already stopped flying.

Their farmhouse had never felt so small; had never felt so scary. She looked around, knowing this was likely the last time she would ever see the only home she had ever known. Details that shouldn't have been important caught her eye and gave her pause: a photograph on the wall of her, Cheyenne, and her parents all smiling at the beach on a vacation to the Okanagan; a pencil sketch Cheyenne had drawn in Art class, stuck to the refrigerator; the coffee stain on the couch her mom had always sworn she'd remove when she had some time. Memories, fragments of her home—all crying out to her, willing her to stay, just a moment longer; hinting that if she could hold out for a few more minutes, perhaps she could save it all.

A rough hand wrapped around her bicep, and another scooped up Cheyenne as the officer whisked both sisters out the door.

Annika quickly forgot the bruising to her arm once she

was outside. Flames towering overhead, the urgency quickly dawned on her.

She looked back to the farmhouse one last time, reminiscent of the biblical story of Sodom and Gomorrah, when Lot's wife couldn't help but look back at the city about to be destroyed for its sins.

Annika didn't turn to salt, like in the scripture, but her mind turned to stone. The only life she had ever known was about to be engulfed in flames, and her parents were not with her.

Cheyenne screamed beneath the officer's left arm, crying out that she didn't want to go. In another instant, a flaming tree silenced her cries as it crackled and then crashed at the edge of the driveway.

The officer threw them inside his SUV before rushing to the driver's side, slamming the vehicle into drive, and hitting the gas. Rocks and gravel flew as the wheels found traction. RCMP vehicles were all manually driven, as they needed the ability to adjust their course at a moment's notice to navigate Canada's precarious rural terrain.

"Where's Mom?" Cheyenne cried.

"Mom and Dad are going to meet us at the bus station," Annika said, though she knew it was a lie. Their parents had gone to the pasture to let the cattle out. They'd believed that if the gate was unlocked, the cows could flee to safety. The AI systems had told them they had two hours before the fire would reach the edge of their land. That was twenty minutes ago, and now their farm was up in flames. By the looks of things, their home would soon be gone, too.

The drive from the burning farmstead was the stuff of nightmares—an apocalyptic hellscape on both sides of the road. Flames engulfed trees on either side, endless fire illuminating the night sky. Annika could see firetrucks, their emergency lights on. Nobody had to tell her they were leaving, too. When even the emergency services were attempting to escape the fire, there wasn't much hope for those who remained.

The officer had grabbed his radio while Annika focused on the flames and was now hurriedly speaking into it. "I managed to get the Phillips's kids out. The parents were apparently trying to free their livestock."

A garbled answer came back through the radio, but Annika couldn't make it out over the noise from the road.

"I dunno, sir," the officer replied. "We barely got out. There are flames everywhere. I don't think anyone expected this thing to move so fast. I'm bringing them to the evac center."

"The drones might still lead them out, right?" Annika asked, clinging to a desperate hope.

"I hate to tell you this, kid," the officer said, "but the drones aren't in the area anymore. They had to clear out ahead of the water bombers."

Annika's heart sank. The officer's eyes met hers in the rearview mirror.

"Maybe they'll be waiting for you at the evacuation center."

Annika knew there was no chance of that; her parents wouldn't have left her and Cheyenne, no matter what. The technology they had depended on to keep them safe had let them down. The warning systems that were supposed to let them know how much time they had before the fire descended and the drones that were supposed to lead them to safety had both failed them.

Tears streamed down her face.

Technology had made her parents' farm nearly obsolete, and now it had allowed them to be killed. Corporate farms had been buying up the land around their property over the past few years. The giants could run the land cheaper and more efficiently with AI-managed systems. There was no way they could have competed. And now the little farm her parents had clung to had burned—along with her parents.

Annika held Cheyenne close to her. Cheyenne, somehow staying quiet and calm, her head resting on her chest, had wrapped her little arm around Annika's neck. Her younger sister likely didn't grasp the gravity of the situation, but her eyes were wide, staring into the flames that threatened to consume them.

Annika resisted the urge to scream. Her entire world had just been turned upside down because the stupid bots had given up on her parents. The human police officer had barely got them out alive, but he still came, despite it being near hopeless. Annika knew a little about how the AI drones worked. They would have calculated that there was a better chance of being destroyed than saving her parents. They wouldn't even have tried.

The drones could have helped her parents, but instead they'd left. Even at seventeen, Annika knew that, given the chance, no human would have done that.

Tears flowed down her cheeks in a steady stream, pooling in Cheyenne's hair. Her sister was her responsibility now.

# Chapter Seven

Cheyenne
Grand Kawa Hotel — Las Vegas, 2052

CHEYENNE PHILLIPS HAD BEEN in the middle of an important quest when the power went out.

The hour of reserve battery built into the Cyber Dynamics Roam One gaming console connected to her eyepiece ensured she didn't notice at first. Engrossed in the open world narrative of *CyberQuest 2177*, it wasn't until her device had winked out due to low battery that she realized their room was without power.

Ember, their Keeper robot—her *nannybot*, as Cheyenne liked to call it—stood in front of the door to the hotel hall, its pale white arms crossed and orange eyes glowing in the slightly darkened room. Even with daylight streaming through the open blinds over the window, Ember's lighting produced an eerie glow. Cheyenne had only ever seen the bot like this when the power was out—it was in emergency mode.

Without the distraction of her game, Cheyenne focused on the surrounding room. Nothing seemed to have changed, except for Ember's eyes. Leftover containers from lunch had been piled on the counter, and the smell of sushi masked that of the fresh paint and new carpets. The suite Annika's work had provided was basically a full apartment and was nicer than their own place back home. Everything on the Las Vegas Strip was so fantastical, it was like a dream to Cheyenne. The novelty of it all gave the impression that everything was new, despite some hotels being over a century old.

Ember, the only familiarity in the room, had always been a point of uniqueness in Cheyenne's life. Robots weren't common in the rural farmland of Saskatchewan, and for someone to have their own personal robot was even rarer. Here, though, robots ran every hotel. They weren't just the order-taking machines most restaurants had or the self-checkouts the elderly complained were stealing the jobs the community's youth no longer wanted; here, there was a robot for *everything*. In this world, Cheyenne was no longer a freak, no longer a symbiont who relied on her bot because of dead parents. In this world, *everyone* depended on the bots. It made Cheyenne feel like she had been living in the wrong place all these years. Here, in Las Vegas, nobody batted an eye at the Keeper's presence.

The only exception were the people outside, their crudely painted signs protesting the bots. They were angry the bots had put them out of work.

Ember had been with her and Annika since the fire. Cheyenne still woke in the night with nightmares, reliving moments from that day, despite it being seven years ago. In some ways, it felt as though Ember had been with them her entire life—and in some ways, it had been. She could barely remember what the first half of her life had been like; what two parents watching over her instead of a bot had meant. What it would be like with a complete family.

"Ember?" she asked. "What's happening? Why is the power out?"

The room she had been stuck in for most of the week had been a bit boring, but at least she'd been able to pass the time with her video games, and there was always her schoolwork. Annika had been so excited to take Cheyenne with her, but her sister had forgotten to mention she'd be alone most of the time.

It annoyed Cheyenne that she still had to attend online classes. Annika had promised her a holiday.

The clock on the wall showed 4:45 p.m. As was often the case, Cheyenne had lost track of time while playing *CyberQuest*. Her classes had ended a few hours ago.

Anni should be back by now, she thought.

Her stomach growled, and Cheyenne greedily eyed the containers Ember had brought up for lunch. The smell of sushi still lingered, but the containers had been emptied hours ago. She had made supper reservations at the Eiffel Tower, but there were still a few hours to go. She'd need something to eat before then.

"The resort systems are out," Ember replied. "The cause of the outage is unknown. It is being advised for all guests to stay in their rooms, and not to leave the hotel until the power is restored."

Cheyenne rolled her eyes. Hopefully it would be back on before supper. Maybe Annika would grab something for her on the way back to the room.

Ember was one of the most humanlike robots Cheyenne had ever seen. From the neck up, Ember looked almost the same as Cheyenne did. Only her bone white skin and glowing eyes betrayed her. Otherwise, the bot's flesh was lifelike.

Cheyenne struggled to let herself admit it, but the bot could even have been considered beautiful. Its long, unnaturally orange hair was enough to catch someone's eye, but it wouldn't take an observer long to establish her as an android. The otherwise robotic appearance of orange panel lighting sealed the deal for anyone who looked past what could be an eye-catching orange dye job.

"Ember, the battery for my eye-piece is dead. Can you message Annika and ask her to bring something to eat on her way?"

"There is an error trying to connect to the communications network," the bot replied. "I'm unable to send a message to Annika."

"*Ugh.*" Cheyenne flopped herself on the bed. It seemed like she was going to have to wait.

At first, Cheyenne had been skeptical of Ember's presence in their home. Annika had blamed the drones for letting her parents die, then her older sister had been outraged that someone thought the bot could replace their mother and father. The android would offer no love, no warmth. It absolutely would not happen.

In the weeks that followed, Annika struggled to keep up with the responsibility parenthood required. Barely an adult, and unable to find a full-time job to support them, it was either accept the help the government was offering or risk losing her sister to foster care.

Cheyenne could tell it angered her sister, though. Bots had let their parents die, and now one was her primary guardian.

Some big company had bought the farm their family had run for generations, but their parents had owed so much on it trying to keep up with the latest technology that Annika and Cheyenne had barely received enough from the sale to provide their parents with a proper burial. Or that was about as much as she understood about what had happened, anyway.

"Do you know how long the power will be out for?" Cheyenne asked, wondering what the odds were of having to forgo dinner altogether.

"There is no estimated time for restoration of power to Las Vegas, Nevada," Ember said, vocalizing a report it was receiving from her network. Her systems were connected to municipal data points, and she could provide detailed statuses provided by emergency services. At least the information network appeared to be operational.

Cheyenne got off the bed and went to the bathroom, plugged the tub, and turned the water on. She didn't know if the same rules applied in Las Vegas, but on the farm, she was responsible for filling the tub in an emergency. That way, if the supply was disrupted, there would be water available to drink or flush the toilet.

Cheyenne wondered whether there was anything else she could do in this foreign locale. At home, she'd gather candles and flashlights and ensure the radio batteries were charged. Here, there were none of those things, and she felt oddly disconnected from the outside world.

Ember stood blocking the doorway, as if Cheyenne might decide to make a run for it.

Cheyenne moved to the window, looking past the blinds for the first time that day. The size of the protests had increased compared with previous days. It was mesmerizing to watch, as she had never seen that many people all in one place before. Even Saskatoon, the nearest center to their small town, was a tiny place compared to Las Vegas.

A sea of people swarmed the street, easily triple the size of the previous day. Heads swam in an ocean of bodies. She could make out the fists of protesters being held in the air, along with large paper signs, the slogans of which were too small to read from her forty-eighth-floor window.

Cheyenne didn't need to see the text to know they were

angry about the country's current unemployment issue. Even at her age, Cheyenne hadn't been able to escape the news broadcasts filled with people proclaiming injustice. A prime example of the source of the protester's frustration being that the bots ran the entire Kawa hotel. Part of Cheyenne knew it was bad the people weren't working any longer, but part of her also knew this was the future. Ember had repeatedly proven she was more capable than most human guardians would have been.

On a much smaller scale, even Saskatoon had seen its share of protests as people lost their jobs. Rideshare drivers, restaurant and retail workers, even most of the jobs at the local banks had been eliminated over the past few years. Cheyenne didn't really pay attention to most of it, but it had affected her directly when her school was forced to close due to budget cuts, and all her classes had moved online.

Red and blue lights flashed at one edge of the Strip. Cheyenne had seen officers lining the sidewalk over the last few days, but if they were in front of the Kawa today, the rest of the crowd swallowed them. She could, however, make out several who stood in front of one of the neighboring resorts, one of them holding their radio mouthpiece up and speaking frantically, his arms flailing in panic.

Another officer grabbed their hat and turned toward the crowd. Security bots had set up a barricade in front of the hotel entrance. Protesters pushed up against it, and Cheyenne realized they weren't letting anybody into the hotel at all, not even its guests.

What if they had trapped Annika out on the street?

Cheyenne couldn't see the entrances to other hotels nearby well enough to determine whether the same was true at all resorts, but it did explain why the crowds were so much larger than before.

"Ember," she asked, "why aren't they letting people back inside?"

"All resorts are under lockdown until the power is restored," Ember answered. The bot didn't move from her position by the door. "Nobody may enter or leave."

The bot was acting strange. Ember was a bot, but it wasn't typically so cold and distant. It stood by the door, staring at nothing, a vacant look in its eyes.

"What's going on?" Cheyenne insisted.

The bot's eyes pulsed orange, but it didn't respond.

"*Ugh!*" Cheyenne rolled her eyes, flailing her arms in exaggerated exasperation. "If you're malfunctioning, I'm going to go find Annika. She's probably stuck outside, trying to get in."

She pushed herself past the bed, slipped on her sandals, and stuck the hotel keycard into the pocket of her denim shorts.

Cheyenne folded up her eye-piece and put it in the pocket of her denim shorts. Maybe there was a charging station somewhere else she could use.

Ember was taller than her and didn't have a wide figure, but somehow the bot had positioned itself in such a way to remove any access to the door Cheyenne might have had.

Cheyenne had never seen the bot behave in this way; it was as though it wasn't concerned with Cheyenne's presence any longer, as if standing in front of the door had become Ember's sole task.

Cheyenne stepped to duck beneath Ember's arm and work herself around the bot's white frame.

With the subtlest of movements, Ember moved to fill the gap she sought to take advantage of.

"*Ugh!*" she exclaimed again. "Come on, Ember! Let me out. I need to find Annika."

"I cannot let you leave," Ember stated. The robot's eyes were incapable of empathy.

"Well, I'm not going to be stuck here without food while Annika's trapped outside!" Cheyenne protested. "I need to find her and get something to eat."

"It is not safe to leave," Ember said. "Please do not protest, Cheyenne. I cannot let you leave until it is time."

Time for what?

Cheyenne rolled her eyes and tried to evade the bot once again. This time, a cold synthetic arm reached out, grabbed Cheyenne around the waist, and tossed her forcibly onto the bed.

Chapter Eight

Terre

THE MUSIC HAD STOPPED, the table games abruptly ended, and the slot machines powered down with a buzz that faded within seconds. Terre could make out the faint whirring of guests cashing out their winnings, the one action the machines would allow guests to perform before they powered off completely.

Something was wrong.

The casinos usually opened their doors during a power outage. It allowed ventilation through the building, besides encouraging patrons not to be a fire hazard.

Jerry's eyes lit up, their purple glow now more apparent in the dim lighting. "Can I pour you another drink?" he asked.

Terre looked down at his half-drunk scotch. The thought of another was appealing, but nanobots or not, he didn't know how far he should push his luck on his new company's tab. Besides, he felt as though he needed to focus. He'd give the nanos a chance to work their magic before continuing to imbibe. Between Fredricks's call, the media coverage of the rogue Sentinels in New York, and mysterious lockdowns being imposed on other cities, Terre was inherently wary of what the power outage might mean.

"None for me," Terre answered.

"I'll take another," Hailey said, tapping the edge of her glass with her newly manicured nails, a devilish smile on her face.

Bots still moved across the hotel floor, liberally filling the drinks of patrons. There was no reason for people to lose their shit as long as the alcohol kept flowing and the games kept playing.

And yet something itched at the back of Terre's mind. This was more than the simple outage it appeared to be.

In his pocket, Terre's phone buzzed. He looked at its screen and immediately excused himself from the bar.

"I'll be right back." He nodded to Hailey and slipped his phone back into his pocket. Hailey didn't seem to have any qualms about listening in to his conversations, and he had a feeling this was one call he didn't need anyone eavesdropping on. "Would you mind watching my things?"

Hailey nodded as his cell continued to buzz against his thigh. The atmosphere in the casino had noticeably changed, now subdued when compared to the deafening roar of music and excitement that had filled it only moments ago. But, though not as intrusive as before, it was hardly quiet. Chatter still filled the hall as patrons happily wandered the floor, content to wait for the lighting to be restored.

The call emphasized the abnormality of the afternoon outage. Fredricks calling for the second time was peculiar enough, but, more ominously, when Terre had looked down at his screen to take the call, it had indicated there was no service.

The looks on nearby faces, all gazing questioningly at their eye-pieces and cell phones, confirmed what Terre's phone reported. No cell service, yet Fredricks's call was still getting through.

Terre wasn't going to question what military magic was at play, and, regardless, he didn't want to draw attention to himself.

The nearest washrooms were, of course, hidden around a few convoluted corners of the resort, but as he had been staying there a few days, Terre had a rough idea of where he was going. Rather than the big, open bathrooms most casinos had, the Kawa had installed individual stalls with a larger communal room for the sink. It kept them from needing to gender the bathrooms, and it felt a little more posh than the giant cavern of urinals of other men's rooms.

Emergency lighting cast an eerie blue hue on spider plants, bonsai trees, and other greenery propped around the room. Silver sinks reflected the dim glow, reflecting subdued patterns onto mirrors hung above them.

The bathroom stalls were situated down a small hall off to the side. They weren't completely soundproof, but the full-length doors to the stalls would grant him a bit of privacy.

Terre wrapped his hand around the handle of a random stall door and closed it behind him, blanketing him with darkness.

It seemed like an oversight not to include emergency lighting in the stalls, as had been done in the common area, but it would have to do. Terre took out his phone, the light of the device providing enough luminescence for him to find and take a seat before answering.

"Terre here," he said, keeping his voice low.

"Hoffman," the familiar voice replied. "Took you long enough."

"Well, I had a feeling I wouldn't want to be on the casino floor for whatever it is you're about to tell me."

"Is the power out there?" Fredricks asked.

"Do you really need to ask? What's going on, Fredricks?"

"Listen," Fredricks said, his voice a low growl. "The AI has hijacked the power grid. Power's gone out in thirteen western states, and we don't have a way to bring it back on."

"All right. So, call the FERC. Why are you telling *me* this?"

"I told you we might need you, wise-ass," said Fredricks.

"Yeah, that was barely an hour ago. I remember."

"Turns out whatever you and the kid did at Berkeley stopped the Sentinels from targeting us, but it didn't bring them back under our control. The guys over at R&D thought they had a handle on them, but their success has been intermittent. We manage to control them, but it seems only if they *allow* it. Some have started acting on their own initiative again. The few in New York made the news, but there's been a media ban on running stories of any others. Social media sites have been taken down to minimize the damage, but it is only a matter of time before word spreads. The last thing we need is panic.

"There's something going on near your current location, and I'm being tasked with finding out what it is and why."

Terre was losing his patience. The whisky, still being filtered by the nanobots, was going to his head. He was tired and wanted nothing more to do with the military's failed experiment.

"What are you getting at?"

"All hell is about to break loose. What I'm about to tell you is classified, Hoffman, so keep it zipped. Specifically, the bots have been up to something in the Nevada desert, near the Hoover Dam, for about a week. Somehow, they managed to fly under everyone's radar until now."

"What do you mean, 'up to something?'" Terre asked. "Like weapons of mass destruction something, or bizarre robot sex cult something?"

"To be honest, we have no idea. The only eyes we could get on the area tell us they're building something."

"The dam's crawling with tourists. How did nobody notice? A worker? A tour bus operator? Nobody?"

"You were stationed in Guam for too long." Sarcasm dripped from Fredricks's tone. "It's all automated now. The whole dam operates itself. A systems analyst shows up once a week to ensure everything is updated and running as it should, but otherwise nobody works there anymore."

"What about the tourists? Nobody saw anything?"

"All tours are driverless and self-guided. They stopped allowing manual drivers in years ago to ease congestion. Tours have been booked solid, but apparently empty buses and vehicles have been driving there. Someone or something tampered with the system to ensure nobody was watching."

"So, *again*, I ask, why are you trying to rope me into this?"

"It's your lucky day, Hoffman. Turns out your new employer, Zatica Industries, operates the dam's systems."

"Well, it isn't yours. I don't start until next week. I'm on vacation."

"You start today."

"Is there really nobody else who can check?" Terre asked. "I'm supposed to be out of the game. Recovering from the last mission you sent me on."

"I wish there was. There's one more thing: Intelligence believes Klein is out there. He's the reason I need *your* help."

Terre swallowed. Kristopher's involvement changed things. "What are you talking about?"

"He's up to something. We've got intel placing him in the area before the satellites blacked out. We suspect he might try to sabotage our recon efforts."

"That doesn't sound like K," Terre replied. "He's a little brash and full of himself, but he's no terrorist."

"That's what we need to determine."

"Wouldn't a tactical force be better equipped? Police? Security?"

"All other resources are currently occupied with a thousand other emergencies. We can only suspect it's something tech related. We need this op to be discreet. Plus, he'll talk to you," Fredricks said. "At least, that's their hope."

Terre sighed. *Not likely.*

"Trust me," Fredricks continued, "from what I'm hearing, you're not going to want to stay in Vegas for long. Something ugly's headed your way. I don't even have details on what it's gonna look like, but the National Guard's involved, and other forces are readying for the worst. You need to leave the city ASAP."

"More rogue drones?" Terre asked.

"I'm not authorized to reveal any further information. But don't waste any time."

Terre sighed. "There are hundreds of people in this hotel, sir. What about them? Should I warn people? Overtake the bots and get out of Dodge?"

"Don't do anything that will incite panic or make things worse. The Guard is on their way; let them deal with the situation on the ground. Start hauling ass to the Hoover Dam. Don't use a driverless or computerized vehicle if you can help it; civilian tech might be compromised. And don't engage with the bots if you don't have to. I'll call you again this evening. I expect you to be mobile by then."

The phone went silent, and Terre knew the man on the other end had hung up. He pocketed the device and put his hands to his forehead, leaning on them as he sat in the dark.

What a nightmare.

Terre didn't know what kind of bullshit move Fredricks had used to co-opt his new position with Zatica, but he wasn't up for playing games. He had no desire to do this again. He was still undergoing therapy from the last mission he'd been sent on. His therapist would kill him if she learned he was heading back into the trauma that had started his descent.

Something ugly's headed your way.

Fredricks's words sunk in, and Terre let out a long sigh. He fought flashbacks from penetrating his thoughts, but he couldn't stop the flashes of orbs reigning fire down on San Francisco. The images filled his vision, piercing through the darkness of the bathroom stall as though the battle surrounded him once more. Was Vegas doomed to suffer the same fate?

As much as he didn't feel like traipsing through the desert, Terre also wasn't keen on being stuck anywhere the bots were about to unleash holy terror. If the National Guard was moving in, hopefully that meant they could evacuate, or at least secure, the city's inhabitants before it was too late.

A fist banged twice on the door. Terre jumped at the sudden noise and vibrations through the toilet seat.

"Hey, buddy!" a man's voice called through the door. "Do you have service? I need to call my wife, and nobody else has a signal."

"Err, no," Terre replied. "No service here, either." It was the truth, but he couldn't help but glance at his screen, where the 'No Service' message was prominently displayed.

"Don't lie to me!" The voice immediately turned angry. "I heard you talking to someone! I need to tell my wife I can't get her from the airport!" The man gave another punch to the door for good measure.

Terre was grateful it wasn't made of glass.

He sighed as he stared into the darkness. He had no interest in fighting over a cell phone.

"I'm sure, given the circumstances, she'll figure it out," he replied.

"You don't know my wife."

Terre couldn't very well explain why he'd been talking to himself in the bathroom stall, but perhaps if the man saw he was telling the truth about having no service, he'd go searching for someone else who could help him.

"Hang on, buddy," Terre replied, rubbing his temple. "I'll come out and prove it."

He stood up and fumbled for the door handle, missing a few times and brushing his hand against the door's wooden surface. Eventually, he found it and twisted the lock.

The man who stood outside couldn't have been more than five feet tall. He was stout, hadn't shaved in at least three days, and though he couldn't have been older than his midtwenties, his hairline was steadily retreating. His face contorted in such a way that Terre was sure the man was preparing himself for a fistfight.

"Easy, fella," Terre said. He held up his hands, facing outward, his phone in one and with the screen lit, as a peace offering. "See for yourself. No bars."

The man's face contorted further; a quivering chin evolved into a full body shake as if his hopes were being crushed in a vice-like grip. His fists balled and Terre braced himself, waiting for them to come flying. The stall behind him wasn't large enough to make either a stand or to retreat.

Instead, the man turned and threw his fist at the opposing wall, a fist-shaped dent forming instantly on its surface.

"Dammit!" the man shouted.

Terre winced at the reaction but breathed a sigh of relief that the anger hadn't been directed at him.

"Aggression detected." Mechanical voices rolled down the hall, accompanied by lights flashing on top of square units. "Hostile force detected."

A human security guard followed close behind. The dark-skinned man was clean-cut and clean-shaven. His skin still had its youthful softness, evidence that the man hadn't yet endured the experiences that would inevitably harden him. If the bots didn't replace him completely before that happened.

"What seems to be the problem?" the guard asked. His hands flexed around his belt, ready to draw a weapon if things went south.

"I think we're okay," Terre said, holding his hands out and eyeing the aggressor, unsure if they actually were. "My buddy here is just a little stressed."

The guard's eyes surveyed the dented wall where the man's fist had landed. "You punched the wall?" he asked incredulously.

The man looked at his knuckles and then at the wall, as if only then realizing what he had done. He looked back at the guard, rage still burning in his eyes.

"Are you taking orders from them now? *Traitor!* A slave to the bots while the rest of us can't feed ourselves. And now they have us caged in here like animals!"

The guard put his hands in front of him, motioning for the man to settle.

"Take it easy. We've only been without power for about an hour. It's going to be okay."

"Why can't we leave?" the man said, his voice pleading and his eyes wide. "I need to get to my wife."

"As soon as we have more information, we'll let you know. Until then, you need to relax ..."

"You're not listening!" the man snapped, lunging forward toward the guard.

Before Terre could even comprehend what was happening, the two square bots darted in front of the man and ejected two rounds of metal binding. The constraints wrapped around his body, incapacitating him before gently lowering him to the floor.

"Aggression detected," one bot said. "You will be restrained and held until the police arrive."

A metal platform extended from their bases, sliding underneath the man's constrained body; one beneath his torso, and one beneath his legs. The platform lifted him a few inches off the ground, and the bots carried him out of the hall toward an unseen destination.

"Are you okay?" the guard asked, turning to Terre.

Curses were still audible from within the casino as the security bots wheeled away.

"I'm fine. But I can't say the same for the wall." Terre rubbed his neck. "It's a good thing those bots act fast."

The guard pointed to a corner of the ceiling. "The whole network's connected. AI and facial recognition ensures there's no room for error. The system is constantly monitoring the entire building for acts of aggression, cheating, pickpockets—you name it. They're on any incident within a few minutes."

"Yet the Kawa still employ human guards? Seems like they've got more eyes on the place than we'd ever hope for."

"Let's just say the bots still aren't great at reasoning with people. Most incidents occur after a few too many drinks. I mostly talk people down if I can; convince them it's time to call it a night. Bots haven't quite reached the level of finesse that requires. Not yet, at least."

"Lucky for you." Terre nodded. "Thanks for stepping in."

"Don't mention it. And don't worry about the wall. The maintenance bots will repair that overnight."

Terre rubbed his neck again, shaking off the encounter. It wasn't a good sign that tensions were already rising. Terre guessed there was more than one couple, or family, separated between the resorts. That guy might have been on the extreme end of how people were handling things, but he was clearly not alone in his assessment of the situation. Terre could see it in the eyes of the patrons who wandered the floor, pulling up their eye-pieces or looking at their watches.

Some continued to hold their phones in the air as if hoping to receive service. In essence, he stood in a room full of inebriated gamblers who were used to being connected every moment of the day.

Terre needed to focus on his next course of action. If he were to go along with Fredricks's request—and he still wasn't sure whether he was going to—he had been instructed to leave the city, but Terre wasn't even sure how he would leave the building. There were at least a hundred hotel guests and visitors surrounding the main exit, hoping to get out. Terre was certain most of them weren't staying at the Kawa and that they had no way of getting back to wherever they were staying on the Strip. It would be a mess even if the hotel's doors opened, and Terre was confident they wouldn't anytime soon.

Terre scoffed. An hour. Humanity had trained itself to be so attention deficit that even an hour of waiting without distraction was too much to handle. Not that he could congratulate himself too much on that front; his skin itched on account of not being able to check his phone. But he had nobody to call; nobody to check in on. And Terre definitely didn't want to talk to the only person in the world who knew where he was.

Terre checked his watch. It was nearly six o'clock. No wonder people were getting agitated. If the casino didn't have a plan to feed these people, things would get ugly in a hurry. There had to be restaurants open, maybe a buffet. Even if the Kawa was running on pure backup generators, they had to make provisions for food. With the thousands of tons of food Vegas went through in a day, they wouldn't want it all to go bad. Then again, delivering it to thousands of agitated guests might be more of a challenge than he realized.

Terre's stomach growled at the thought of the buffet, but there'd be no time to stop for a snack.

He wished Fredricks had given him a little more insight about what was going on. As it was, he was being sent blind into a potential replay of the nightmare in San Fran.

He eyed the robot bartender, Jerry, as he returned to his seat at the Sakana Tamago bar. The bot wore an unnecessary black vest, its lights glowing the faint purple that doubled as emergency lighting. Maybe it would have looked better with hair, but Terre didn't think so.

Jerry, of course, hadn't moved since he'd left. Thankfully, neither had the woman who Terre had entrusted to watch his seat.

"You really want to become one of them?" he asked Hailey, motioning to Jerry with one hand as he punched his access code into the datapad with the other.

Hailey was casually watching the growing agitation around her. The bar had filled since he'd left. The allure of the table games seemed to have worn off for some, and wasting some time at the bar seemed as good an alternative as any. The bar menu was light on food, but anything would be better than nothing.

"Not one of them," she replied as she set down her Cucumber Cosmo. "Better. Still human, but more. There's nothing saying we can't improve ourselves by integrating with what we've learned about robotics. We use so much of the technology anyway; we just don't think of it in that way. Smartphones, eye-pieces … Hell, most people already connect their brains to the network via implants. Imagine if we could handle and streamline the information for the collective good? And on top of that, we could ensure our bodies didn't age. The technology already exists; medics use nanobots in surgeries already. Why wait until an emergency? Why not install them pre-emptively? We have a way to delay, if not cure, the disease of aging. Don't we deserve that freedom?"

Terre stared into the vacant eyes of the clientele at the slot machines. So many of them had nothing to live for. Bots had stolen their livelihoods; stolen their dreams. He knew many were here on a last-ditch effort, gambling away the little pensions they had or their UBI, if they were lucky enough to live in a state that provided one. There were people, both within and outside these walls, who didn't know where their next meal would come from.

"You really think humanity deserves to live forever?" Terre pressed. "We barely make it to a hundred and look at the mess we make. The robots have only just begun to make us obsolete and look at what's happened. Suicide rates are at an all-time high, while others," he nodded toward the slot machines, "Others are just waiting to die."

Hailey crossed her legs and took another sip of her drink. She followed Terre's gaze out onto the casino floor, as if considering his point.

Terre's skin itched; he, too, was considering the point Hailey had made. He had been one of the few recipients of the experimental nanobot injections. He wasn't sure if the tech swimming around his veins made him fortunate or not. They sounded great in theory. Even as he spoke, they were repairing cells, restoring him to a state of being he had barely known in his twenties. But was this really the future of humanity? The extension of life via integrated cyberware? He was unsure if it was a power the masses could handle.

"Leaving so soon?" Hailey asked as he set the datapad down.

"I have some business I need to take care of," he said.

"I thought you were on vacation?" she asked, stirring her drink.

"Yeah, so did I."

"Work taking you out of the hotel? With everything that's going on?"

"Yeah," he said. "It's related to whatever's going on." Terre didn't know how much he could tell a perfect stranger, but he had little information himself, so it wasn't like he could spill any secrets. Besides, he hadn't decided yet if he was actually going anywhere, but the air within the Kawa was getting stale and, at the very least, he'd be happy to get outside.

"It was nice meeting you," he said. "Enjoy the rest of your time in Vegas."

"We'll have to see about that. I'm coming with you," she said. "This hotel is getting stuffy."

Chapter Nine

Terre

It SEEMED to Terre that neither Fredricks nor Hailey realized the exits to the Kawa had been sealed, and that getting out of the hotel would not be as simple as it sounded. He didn't exactly encourage Hailey to join him, but he didn't have the heart to tell her no, either.

Maybe it was the scotch, but it was nice to finally have a bit of company.

Terre had to dissuade Hailey from trying to head to the main lobby. He wondered how many of those Cucumber Cosmos she had consumed *before* she'd sat down at the bar. The crowd, eager to get out, had only grown, and though it wasn't visibly obvious from where they had been seated, Terre could hear the commotion in the main lobby growing as they made their way across the casino floor.

"We won't be able to get out that way," he said.

Hailey raised a questioning eyebrow. "You're not trying to get me back to your room, are you, Mr. Secret Service?"

Terre scoffed. "You're the one that wanted to come along, remember? The main exits are sealed. You can see the back of the crowd spilling into the casino." He pointed to the edge of the floor, where dozens of people were struggling to push forward. "I'm going to find another exit. Up to you if you want to join me or not."

Terre thought he might have imagined a slight frown on her face, but she nodded.

"All right, Secret Service man. Lead the way."

They crept through the casino. There was no real reason to hide their intentions—nobody would have noticed them—but if there was another exit, Terre didn't want it to be overrun by people jumping at the chance of freedom, bots, or both. If Fredericks was right, they had twenty-four hours before shit hit the fan.

And if Terre knew Fredricks, it was probably less.

Agitated guests eyed the crowded restaurants encircling the floor. They were getting hungry, and if they couldn't leave, it meant they'd have to be fed at the resort. But judging by the lines outside their doors, it didn't look like the restaurants were accepting new patrons.

Terre's belly rumbled at the thought of dinner, and he pushed the sensation aside. He'd grab something on the way if he saw an opportunity, but he knew it might be a while. Sweat beaded on his forehead. The last of the air conditioning was fading. The time for civility was running short.

The sounds of chips falling, cards shuffling, and dice landing on tables still permeated the casino. But the cheers had become muted behind an ever-growing roar of human agitation. Table games could only distract all but the most dedicated gamblers for so long without food.

Terre did his best to keep to the edges of the floor, shuffling around the larger groups of people. He cursed under his breath as he wound past dozens of angry patrons. He wanted to warn them; to let them know that doom was on its way. So many people just awaited their doom. But he didn't truly know *what* was about to happen. Fredricks was right, however; warning them would do little but incite panic. Bots had blocked the door, and it was already unlikely that he would be able to exit undetected. If he caused a riot, there would be no way he'd get out, and they would all die in here.

At least if he was able to figure out whatever harebrained quest Fredricks was sending him on, there was a chance this would be the most inconvenienced the crowd would become.

Doubtful, he thought.

Either way, there was nothing Terre could do to help the hotel guests, except trust that whatever Fredricks was after would benefit them. The National Guard would be more prepared to deal with any threat that might descend on the city, and hopefully they'd be in a position to protect the people within the city's limits.

Right now, Terre had only one concern—to get out of the city.

His gait slowed as he came to realize the thoughts that passed through his head. He had made the decision to venture out into the desert and hadn't even realized it. Damn Fredricks and his manipulative bullshit! K was certainly not Terre's responsibility. And an impending attack on Vegas would only be his problem as long as he remained within the city.

If he could get out of the hotel, he could just run. Terre had been wanting to run from responsibility—to run from *life*—ever since the attack on Guam, and now was possibly the chance to do it. His cell phone weighed heavily in his pocket. He could toss it in the nearest garbage can and disappear. If ever there was an opportunity to vanish off-grid, an attack on national security would provide him an opportunity like nothing else could.

Terre kept the thought to himself. For now, he just had to get out of the building.

They walked past the elevators, where another sizable crowd had congregated. Half of its number appeared to be considering whether it was worthwhile to take the stairs to their rooms. Terre wondered how many of them could make the trip if they had to traverse more than a few floors. Likely there were a few who had simply resigned to wait until the power came back on. Some sat on the floor along the wall, the elderly and the otherwise unable to climb stairs, forced to wait for the power to bring back the only viable way to return to their rooms.

"I'm on the thirty-eighth floor," Terre said, pointing to the crowd. "If you want to go back to my room, we have a lot of stairs to climb."

He didn't slow, but he caught the slack-jawed look on Hailey's face as she surveyed the crowd surrounding the elevator doors, waiting for their release.

"It might be worth it," she said with a smirk. "How do people get into their rooms with the power out, anyway? All the rooms use electronic keycards."

"The keycard locks have battery backups," he replied. "As long as the hotel checks the batteries frequently, there shouldn't be any issues."

Terre subconsciously felt for his own card in his pocket. He'd love not to abandon his belongings on the crazy expedition to flee the city, but he wasn't going to climb thirty-eight flights of stairs if he didn't have to, either.

The sound of Hailey's heels clicked behind him.

"You're going to need to lose the heels if you want to tag along," he said.

Hell, why was *he letting her tag along?*

He slowed half a step to let her keep up. She walked impressively fast for someone in heels, but it wouldn't be enough. Hailey stumbled slightly before opting to take them off, sliding the shoes from her feet in one swift motion and hardly slowing down before shuffling across the carpet in bare feet.

"Hun, do you mind telling me *exactly* what I'm signing myself up for?" The skin of her feet revealed tan lines, presumably from flip-flops she'd recently worn at the pool. "I enjoyed having a drink with you, but something doesn't feel right about all this. You seem to have a plan, and I don't think it ends with us leaving the hotel."

"I think you've got good instincts," he said. *Definitely the whisky.* "Right now, I'm just trying to find a way out of the Kawa. If I go along with what my former employer wants, then I'm leaving the city. If that happens, you're welcome to join me. But I don't know what I'm dealing with yet."

"I don't think I'm going to want to be in Vegas for much longer, anyway," she said.

Terre studied her from the corner of his eye. The woman must have been more intuitive than she seemed. There was something she wasn't telling him.

"Who did you say you worked for?" he asked. "Creating cyborgs is pretty specialized work. You really believe it's a good idea to mix organic life with technology?"

"I wasn't kidding. Human cybernetic integration is the future. You think it's a gigantic leap to go from an eye-piece to an implant?"

"I never said I didn't think it was *possible*. I just wonder how good of an idea it is. You work under the assumption we can keep these things under control."

"You should know better than anyone," Hailey replied. "It's just lines of code."

"I *do* know better than anyone," Terre answered. *More than you realize.* "Look at those bots that attacked San Francisco. The ones going rogue in New York? You want something like that in your head, ready to malfunction at any moment? No, thank you."

"It's only a matter of time before it's a reality," Hailey persisted. "More and more people are getting chipped every day. Pretty soon, we'll have the entirety of the world's information at our disposal with no more than a thought. Those who refuse will be left behind; dinosaurs staring at the meteor crashing down, wishing they could've been mammals instead."

"The neuronet has been a pipe dream for decades," Terre replied.

The crowd thinned as Terre and Hailey reached the rear of the building. It seemed most people had become resigned to their fate at the main exit or by complaining to the front desk, which was an effort doomed to frustration since there was only one kiosk manned by a virtual assistant. Yelling at it would be a waste of air. During normal circumstances, everything would have been managed through the datapad in their rooms or an app on their eye-piece.

They came to the end of the room. A faux wall had been set up to separate the main floor from what looked like a construction area. Sheets of industrial plastic hung in the darkness behind the paneled wall.

Terre remembered reading that the casino had plans for expansion, but the work had only just begun. The Kawa had planned for the future promenade to act as a connection between two other nearby resorts. Perhaps this would be their way of getting out.

Terre peered over his shoulder. They were tucked away in shadow, and anybody who wasn't still milling about on the casino floor appeared to be taking their chances at the front. He knew that wouldn't last for long. The more bored, desperate, and inebriated people became, the more willing they'd be to explore.

Terre scanned the ceiling. There were several security cameras, but not nearly as many as there were above the tables and cashiers. Terre wondered if entering the restricted area would be enough incentive for the security bots to intercept them, but there was only one way to find out.

A series of temporary paneled walls had formed a small hallway. To anyone who was looking at the area from across the casino floor, it would have appeared to be a solid wall. But if plans were to connect the building to those behind it, there would have to be an exit, and if luck was smiling on Terre, hopefully the unwatched construction site would provide access outside.

Around the camouflaged corner, a large orange sign hung on the wall:

Restricted Area. Keep Out.

Below that rested a more polite sign, branded with the Kawa logo:

Construction in progress. In order to keep our guests safe, please keep out. Authorized personnel only. Thank you for understanding.

"Are you sure we're supposed to be back here?" Hailey asked, her voice flat and distant, as though she were asking out of obligation but wasn't truly concerned about the answer.

She peered back toward the casino but then ducked behind the row of paneling. Her brown eyes narrowed as she surveyed the half-walls on either side of them. The ceiling must have been twenty feet high, but the walls extended about twelve. Above the unfinished ceiling, pipes and vents had been painted black to make it less obvious there was still work to be done; a harsh, rugged comparison to the sleek, streamlined aesthetic of the rest of the resort.

Terre shook his head at the ridiculousness of their predicament. He'd just wanted a few drinks at the bar; had that been too much to ask? Now, instead, he was a bit lightheaded with a pro-cybernetics groupie in tow, trying to sneak through a construction zone of a Las Vegas casino.

And for what?

Because an old coworker had gone off the deep end after saving the world?

Potentially *saving the world*, he corrected himself.

Terre still couldn't wrap his head around the thought that K could be implicated in something so damaging after all they had gone through. That said, it was nearly certain that the entire Strip was without power, possibly the entire city— and it was all connected to those damn bots.

Terre nearly stopped in his tracks. Perhaps the effects were more widespread than that. There was no way for him to know, unless Fredricks was willing to tell him.

He pushed the thoughts aside for the moment. The only thing that mattered right now was getting out of the building and then finding his way to the dam.

"What are you doing once we get out?" Hailey asked, as if reading his thoughts. "Surely you aren't just going for a stroll in the desert."

"I need to look for someone," Terre answered. "One of my old coworkers has gotten himself into trouble. He's supposedly doing something he shouldn't be at the Hoover Dam. I need to find him, maybe talk him down."

"But you don't work for this company any longer?" The inflection in her voice suggested she was skeptical.

"It's complicated," he said. "My coworker and I shared a traumatic experience. I might be able to reason with him."

Hailey seemed to take it for a reasonable enough answer. Once they were out of the line of sight of the rest of the casino floor, her demeanor shifted. It was almost as if she gained a level of confidence she hadn't had before, straightening her posture, her stride becoming more determined, and her gaze no longer flitting around as if she expected guards to descend on them at a moment's notice.

"You still haven't told me why you're in Vegas," Terre said.

"I told you before," she said. "The same reason as you."

Terre shook his head. *That still isn't an answer.* But he let the matter drop. The woman's business was her own.

They rounded a final corner. Maintenance bots stood scattered across the room, deactivated in the middle of whatever processes they had been following before the lights went out. The subtle glow of their power-saving state gently lit the back room. It appeared even emergency lighting had yet to be installed. One bot was attached to a hydraulic lift, holding ceiling tiles, ready for its ascent to continue installation. Terre wasn't familiar enough with construction to recognize most of the other tasks on display, but it appeared as though everything from drywall to clean-up was being completed. Everything about the Kawa, he reminded himself, was automated.

On the far side of the cavern, Terre could make out two emergency exit signs, one more spot of light and the only sign there was any end to the dark chamber. One sat in the left corner of the facility, the other on the right.

"Left door?" Terre asked, more to himself than to Hailey. His voice echoed faintly through the space. They could hear the faint hum of chatter from the casino behind them, but most of it was muffled by the time it reached them. Compared to the noise and activity of the principal part of the hotel, the back room felt vacant and eerie, as if it had been forgotten and carried only the echoes of humanity.

"How would I know?" Hailey asked, as if offended by the question. "This was *your* idea."

"Feel free to head back if you don't want to be here," Terre said.

Hailey straightened, but her newfound resolve didn't dissipate. "Let's go right," she said.

"Any particular reason?"

She gave a brief shrug. "No, just a feeling."

"You chose right just because I said left, didn't you?"

Hailey shrugged again, a smirk crossing her face. "Maybe."

"All right," he said, shaking his head. "Doesn't matter to me either way. We'll go right. But watch your step; there's construction material everywhere."

"I'm not an idiot," she said harshly.

Terre nodded as he stepped over a box of nails and pushed ahead to the exit on their right.

The bots were industrial models, robotic arms jutting outside of metal boxes in crude imitation of limbs to enable them to perform simple tasks. There was no need to make these units look pretty. Some bore screens, now dim except for a faint black glow and a yellow light indicating they were in standby mode.

Memories of the bots in the halls of the UC Berkeley lab just before K and he had uploaded the Guardian Program bubbled to the surface of Terre's thoughts. Deadened yellow eyes stared back at him, just as they had when the Sentinels had descended upon the campus, firing at the students and shutting down their upload.

Well, before Terre had fired his own weapon, which had shut off the power and caused the upload to terminate prematurely. If the bots were malfunctioning again, it was likely because of his own actions.

These bots were much cruder than their military counterparts, but the nightmares of the past few weeks still haunted him. Faces or without, they still watched and waited. For him to let his guard down. For him to fail.

Out of nowhere, the bots became a whir of activity.

Terre jumped and took two steps back into the shadows, pulling Hailey with him. His heart raced as the lights on the maintenance units brightened and changed from yellow to blue. Their bodies sprang to life and moved from their resting place in the shadows.

Chapter Ten

Terre

TERRE HELD his back as far against the wall as he could manage, reflexively holding Hailey back with one arm. He had no way of telling whether the maintenance bots had any way of detecting them, and he wasn't going to take any chances.

"What's going on?" Hailey whispered, pushing his arm away in annoyance. "They're just construction bots. They won't bother us."

"Just wait," he said. "We're not supposed to be here, remember? This is a restricted area. I don't want to find out the hard way these bots are being hacked."

"Hacked?" she whispered incredulously.

"*Shh!* I'll explain later."

The bots rolled across the floor in unison, lining abreast of one another before advancing. There were at least a dozen forming a wall that rolled across the floor, approaching where they stood.

Hailey gripped Terre's shoulder. "What are they doing?" she whispered.

Terre held a hand up as they inched closer. He didn't

know exactly what he expected, but he'd experienced more than his fair share of militant bots over the past few weeks.

They're just maintenance bots, he reminded himself. *Not Sentinels.*

It was of little consolation knowing that only one of the bots carried a nail gun. Suddenly, letting Hailey tag along didn't seem like the best idea.

Being corralled in the casino doesn't sound any better.

He turned to Hailey, whose grip had left his arm. She moved as if she was going to make a run for it.

"Hang on," Terre said. "They haven't done anything just yet."

"You want us to wait and find out?" she said. Her stance had changed, and determination was now reflected in her eyes. She was no longer the coy transhumanist sitting at the bar.

"Cool it," he said. "You won't make things better if you let them know we're here."

Terre could feel his pulse in his ears.

All I wanted was a drink at the bar.

The bots broke formation and maneuvered into a single file line, pivoting toward the exit at the opposite end of the room. The same exit Terre and Hailey had decided against.

"We should follow them," Hailey offered.

"You serious? That's the *opposite* of what we should be doing."

What is it with this woman? he thought. *One minute, she's cowering in fear; the next, she wants to go after them.*

"Aren't you curious about what they're up to?" she asked. "Maybe they'll lead us out of here."

"Or maybe they're going into storage until the power comes back on."

Terre watched the last of the robotic lights disappear down the hall. The more he thought about it, he supposed

Hailey had a point; seeing where the bots were going made sense, though it was far more likely they'd be led to a maintenance room than outside. Recent events had him jumping at benign machines.

Before he finished deliberating, Hailey strode across the room, keeping to the edge of the wall, as if worried the bots might return.

Terre sighed and shook his head. Any effect the scotch had had on him had now dissipated. The nanobots had quickly metabolized the alcohol. He wished he could say the same for Hailey; the several Cucumber Cosmos were likely affecting her rationale. He had no better options, though. Regardless of what came next, he *had* to find a way out.

Whether Terre wanted to pursue K into the desert or not, he sure as hell didn't want to be stuck in the city if a fresh assault was looming. The sooner he could get out of Vegas and find K, the sooner he could be done with all this shit.

Or so he hoped.

Terre crossed the floor, following Hailey as she disappeared into the darkness of the opposite hall. He wanted to protest but could think of no valid reason to do so. They were, after all, only maintenance bots. The chances of the units turning on them and inflicting any actual damage was minimal. The real threat was behind them: a room full of drunks without power being held against their will, awaiting a fate they didn't expect and didn't deserve. As much as he didn't want to go through the hell he'd faced in San Francisco again, if there was anything Terre could do to save lives, he had to try.

He knew he was stalling, unsure from one moment to the next what course he should follow. But he knew what he *needed,* and he knew he wasn't selfish enough to run while another city faced possible annihilation. He'd do the only thing he could: figure out what K was up to and put a stop to it.

Emergency lighting returned as they traveled deeper into the building. Terre took it as an encouraging sign that the hall must lead somewhere closer to completion, though, in the relative darkness, it was still difficult to discern where the hallways went. The faint blue glow of the lights revealed cold concrete bricks lining the edges of the wall. Empty poster frames stuck out from its surface, likely homes of future adverts for shows or restaurants. Entertainment seemed to be one of the few career choices the bots had yet to overtake. There were select revues and performances that were bot-based—it was easier to rip someone's head off if they were artificial—but the vast majority of people still wanted to see human performers. Bots still lacked the emotional capacity required for live theater.

After turning another corner, the harsh yellow light of the sun illuminated a square panel on a side wall. A double bay door which had been covered in paper now stood wide open, allowing the daylight to penetrate the hallway. Beyond its opening, wooden beams had been neatly stacked in the middle of the uncompleted hall.

The bots must have exited the building here. Which meant they could as well.

Sirens pierced the silence of the hall. Terre cautiously approached the opening and peered out onto the street below. A makeshift ramp led down; only a small metal railing served as a barricade to the drop. Two stories didn't seem like a treacherous height, but a fall would still be disastrous.

"What the hell is going on?" Terre muttered.

On the street below, the maintenance bots rolled along, still in single file. More converged from neighboring side streets, joining the automation parade, all of them heading in the direction of the Strip. Terre guessed there had to be more bots than just those from the Kawa. A variety of iterations of robots and automated vehicles and equipment drove themselves down the road.

The ground vibrated with the activity. Construction machinery was also on the move, driverless forklifts, cranes, loaders, and excavators all making an exodus. It was hard to tell between the resorts exactly where they were traveling to, but they all seemed to be headed east. Toward the Strip, and likely beyond.

Toward the Hoover Dam, he thought. It was impossible to know for sure, but it was far too convenient that the bots were traveling in the same direction he was headed.

Terre couldn't see the Strip from their vantage point, but he could hear the sirens, the gunshots, and the people screaming. It was only a matter of time before the crowds spilled into the side streets. The protests had been bad enough, and the echoes of gunfire suggested things had escalated. What else was going on? Was he already too late? Already there were a few people running in the alleyways, doing their best to avoid whatever mayhem was unfolding.

It was only then that Terre noticed, other than those caravanning down the freeway, there were no cars moving. The cars he could see were parked, many in the middle of the street, their doors flung open, and many had smashed windows.

"The vehicles went out with the power," he thought out loud. "They've all died."

"Local vehicles charge every night. They wouldn't all have run out of power at once," Hailey replied. "How is that possible?"

"Somehow it is," Terre said, pointing to the street. "Come on. Something's going down on the Strip. I don't want to be here when it spills in this direction."

"Well, where's your friend? Where are we headed? Hopefully not another resort."

Terre sighed. He had no idea what was waiting for them. Did he have any right to bring a complete stranger along? Based on what had happened in San Francisco, he would almost certainly be putting Hailey in danger. The heat of the afternoon washed over him as he gazed at the parking garages and maintenance buildings to the rear of the resort. But how could he leave her here knowing that another attack was imminent? It was bad enough there were so many innocents who would be vulnerable when the military bots showed up, but he couldn't tell Hailey not to come with him. He couldn't knowingly send her into the fire, when coming with him might offer a chance of avoiding the attack.

Or we could be heading for something far worse.

"Hoover Dam, I guess." He ran a hand over his head, scratching an itch above his ear.

"The Hoover Dam? What's there?"

Terre paused, considering his response. "*Answers*, hopefully. The coworker I told you about? My previous employer tells me he might be involved in these bots going rogue and, whatever's going on, he's supposed to be at the dam doing it. But I'm still trying to determine how he's connected to all this myself."

Hailey nodded, admirably taking it all in her stride. "We're going to have to cross the Strip at some point," she said, her eyes following the bots that were still visible a block away. "And if things are going to get bad, we might want to do that sooner rather than later. With no traffic, we could follow the freeway past the airport. Maybe we could get a vehicle there?"

"No," he said. "No vehicles. Whatever's hijacked those maintenance bots likely shut down these cars as well. We can't take that chance."

Hailey nodded distantly.

"That doesn't bother you?"

"Like I said," Hailey replied, her eyes still locked on the bots, "I'm guessing I'm not going to want to see what comes next." She turned to him. "Besides, someone has to keep you out of trouble."

Terre couldn't help the smile that crossed his face. "I won't promise what I'm setting out to do won't be dangerous. But I also can't promise staying here will be any safer."

"Well, from what I can tell, I'm going to be in danger no matter what," she said. "Between the gunfire and the malfunctioning tech, my best bet is to keep close to you. But if we're going to keep walking, I'm going to need to find some shoes."

Terre looked down at her bare feet. Hailey had tucked her heels in her purse. He wasn't sure which would be worse.

He cursed under his breath. "The pavement's going to be a hundred and fifty degrees," he said. "We can't go anywhere until you do."

All he could do to gauge what was happening was to survey the noise coming from the next block up the street. The peaceful sway of palm trees next to the resorts gave a false sense of calm.

"There are dozens of stores connected to the resorts along the Strip, but we're not going to get into one any easier than it was to get out of this one."

"Well, we'll just have to figure it out along the way," Hailey said with a smirk, putting her heeled shoes back on her feet. "These will be better than nothing until then. Just don't expect me to be quick, okay?"

Terre sighed, relenting on his earlier thoughts. Could he afford her slowing him down? Surely it would be better if he found K as quickly as possible. What was K up to, and would he be able to talk his ex-colleague down from whatever he was planning? He had no idea what to think anymore.

"Maybe you should stay here, in the city," he said reluctantly. His mind cringed as he spoke the words. "You can head back up to your room and wait out whatever's going on. I'm sure things will be under control soon."

He didn't mean it—and not just the part about things being under control. He didn't want her to stay. He *knew* she shouldn't stay. Fredricks had told him hell was about to break loose. Terre had only just met this woman, but there was something about her that told him there was more to her than she was letting on. He could see it in her eyes, see it in the way she stood—Hailey didn't strike him as someone who was expecting a fleet of robot workers to take off down the interstate. She didn't question him finding K, she didn't question him fleeing the city, and she'd said herself things were quickly going to get ugly.

The more time he spent with her, the more Hailey was turning out to be quite the mystery.

"Hah!" Hailey scoffed. "You won't get rid of me that easily. It's not safe to be here. You said so yourself."

Terre made his way down the metal slotted stairs to street level. Had he convinced her? He had been pretty sure she'd convinced herself.

"Just because I'm wearing heels doesn't mean I can't handle myself."

"Well, if you've convinced yourself to come with me, maybe you *can* help." Terre surveyed the stream of bots, still visible in the distance. "You're an expert in robotics; can you tell me what causes a hundred maintenance and construction bots to get up and roll out of the city on their own?"

Hailey looked at him, puzzled for a moment, as if perplexed by the question.

"No," she finally said, resigned. "My specialism is *human*

integration. But I'm sure there's a simple explanation. Bots are essentially just lines of code. Every action is just a command they've been programmed to perform. Maybe your friend is doing something to their code."

"What do you mean?"

"Think about it. He's supposedly at the Hoover Dam, and the bots that have rolled out of here seem to be going in that direction. What else comes from the dam?" She paused for dramatic effect. "Oh yeah, the power supply for most of the southwestern United States. One flick of a switch and the Strip goes dark. A little convenient, isn't it? Let me guess, your friend is savvy with robots?"

Terre blinked as he pondered Hailey's point. He doubted it would be as simple as flicking a light switch to turn off the Strip's power, but the premise of what she was implying made sense. The tour schedules had been off for weeks—about the same amount of time that Terre had parted ways with the young programmer.

Could K really be behind this?

But why? Did it mean that this had nothing to do with what happened in New York earlier?

"He's one of the best," he said reluctantly.

Hailey tossed her purse over her shoulder with one arm, and they began their way along the sidewalk. "So, how do you know he's not behind all this?"

There definitely *was* more to Hailey than she was letting on. Either that or she was an incredible problem-solver. She'd quickly connected the dots around the young programmer's involvement.

No matter how traumatized K had been after San Francisco, Terre highly doubted he would intentionally do anything to harm anyone. But Terre had no doubt he'd be one of the few capable of hijacking a bunch of bots.

The stream of maintenance bots had moved on, now out

of sight, though the street still rumbled from the greater exodus. A light breeze provided some relief from the heat of the day, now waning as the sun was descending, and palm trees gently waved their boughs in response.

The sirens that could be heard from the direction of the Strip continued to grow louder, and Terre swore the amount of gunfire had increased. Anarchy, it seemed, was already descending. It would be dark in a matter of hours, and whatever the cause of the chaos down the road, he knew he didn't want to be among it when night fell.

Terre grabbed the robot pendant that hung around his neck, rubbing it between his thumb and forefinger as he focused his thoughts. It appeared Fredricks was right—he wouldn't escape whatever turmoil was about to arrive.

Chapter Eleven

Annika

ANNIKA PUSHED her way past the people filling the street with only one thing on her mind—getting to Cheyenne. Between the protesters and the tourists desperate to return to their hotels, the city had descended into madness.

The steady march of weary travelers had disappeared once they'd hit the Strip. A tsunami of hostility and anger had replaced their weariness.

Annika couldn't decide which was cooking her faster: the burning sun beating down on them or the concrete below her feet, radiating the warmth through her shoes.

Her heart pounded as her feet scraped along the sidewalk. It had been over an hour since they'd left the Convention Center. They had yet to find water, and consequently Annika was feeling lightheaded.

"We're never going to get through this," Becky grumbled behind her.

They had left Marlene and Darla behind a half hour ago. The two women had been intent on finding a pool, and other than a sharp concern for their well-being, Annika had no authority to stop them. They'd said their goodbyes, and

Annika had instructed them to drink plenty of water before they had more booze. The two women had laughed off her suggestion and stumbled off into the sea of protesters.

Annika had grimaced as she'd watched the two stumble away. There was nothing she could do for them. The women were adults and could make their own decisions, but she hoped they took her advice for their own sakes. Somehow, she didn't believe they would.

"We have to," she replied to Becky's negativity. "Cheyenne's in our room waiting for me."

Sirens continued to wail in the distance, occasionally peppered with what could have been gunfire, though Annika thought it was more likely to be fireworks. Annika had yet to hear a credible story about what was going on. One thing she had learned was that the power was out for the entire Strip at least, if not the entire city. Flashing neon signs, flashing monitors, and electric displays had all gone black. The hollowness of the cement towers and the faux monuments lining the boulevard were now lifeless and cold.

It wasn't just the power grid. All driverless vehicles in the streets had stalled as well, including those at the Conference Center—a grid of deadened vehicles littering the Strip.

"What about Ember?" Becky asked. "Isn't that what she's there for?"

Annika sighed. Technically, the bot was supposed to look after her sister, to provide her with comfort and companionship; to be a type of surrogate parent. But nothing about what was happening around them seemed right, and the images of deactivated white bots being carried off the streets of New York had been burned into her mind.

She couldn't shake off the way the bots had looked.

They looked just like Ember.

White-paneled bodies and synthetic skin had lined their faces. The resemblance had sent shivers down her spine.

She *had* to get to her sister.

Annika subconsciously looked to the sky. Memories of what she had seen on the news from San Francisco had been plaguing her thoughts all afternoon, and part of her wondered if the same spheroid bots would appear at any moment and level Sin City in a burst of terror from the sky. Would Vegas be the second Gomorrah she'd face?

Shaking off the thought for the hundredth time, Annika forced her gaze back to the crowd before them. Events she wouldn't have been able to fathom a couple of months ago now seemed like a viable threat. Bots had already torn her little family apart once, and she prayed with every fiber of her being that they wouldn't get the chance to finish the job.

"I don't know what to think," she replied. "I just know I need to get back to her. I will not fail my family again."

Annika took two steps forward into the crowd before Becky's hand grabbed her shoulder.

"You know it's not your fault," Becky said. "It's been what? Seven years? You can't keep blaming yourself for their deaths. Twenty-seven people died that night."

Annika rolled her eyes, before casting her gaze to the sidewalk. Becky had been her best friend since the night of the fire, but she didn't need to be lectured about what was or wasn't her fault. She didn't get the call out in time. She could have gone after them. She could have done something. But she hadn't. She wouldn't wait around for something awful to happen to Cheyenne.

Not this time.

"I don't blame myself," she lied. "It's the bots I blame. The system told my parents they had enough time to let the cattle out. If the government hadn't pretended the bots were so damn infallible, my parents wouldn't have taken the chance."

Becky nodded. "You were just a kid," she said, as though she saw through the deflection. "If you'd tried to go after them, you probably would've died yourself, and then where would Cheyenne be?"

Annika pushed the thoughts aside. The strength of the sun was making her feel sick. Even if the power outage was unrelated to the other attacks being reported on the news, the mob was growing more agitated by the second. Who knew what might happen within the hotel?

"Either way, I'm not going to leave the fate of our family to anyone or anything but *me*. I need to get back to her. She's locked away on her own."

Locked away with Ember.

What if the bot malfunctioned in the same way as the ones in New York? Ember had been nothing but helpful to them for the past seven years, but the machine was just a product of its coding. What if something was hacking the bots to make them act out? Annika would never forgive herself if the nannybot they had welcomed into their home turned on her sister.

She *had* to get to Cheyenne.

Bodies blocked her from pushing forward. She had never seen this amount of people before. Hundreds of protesters, tourists, and conference attendees lined the sidewalk, all displaced from their rideshares or other modes of transportation. Empty vehicles rested beside them like discarded skeletons, rendered useless by some invisible hand.

A pedestrian bridge before them crossed the Strip from one hotel to the next, its concrete stairs packed full of people, leading to a suspended arch swarming with even more pedestrians. Protest signs protruded from within the mass, declaring clever slogans such as *Humans, Not Bots* and *They Have No Soul.*

The believers trying to spread their 'truth' were brandishing placards that should have been raised decades ago. The artificial revolution had been brewing for a long time, and few had truly realized the chaos it would sow. It had slowly crept up on them, threatening from the sidelines, erasing the workforce in one industry after another. Now, the disruption was painfully visible. Now, it had stolen the jobs and livelihood of the majority.

Now, it was too late.

Annika sighed. She sympathized with the protesters' sentiment, but humanity had long since let the genie out of the bottle, and there would be no sticking it back in. There were no three wishes. Only the downfall of the middle class.

Farmers had learned the tough lesson years ago; Annika had seen their neighbors' farms fail one after the other. Many got bought out by big corporations who could afford automated equipment. Her parents had been one of the last to hold out until they'd died at the bots' hands.

The bots had had the last laugh.

Security bots appeared to be doing their job: intimidating the crowd. Several four-legged machines—headless robotic dogs deployed by the Las Vegas Police Department —patrolled back and forth, and the beasts were effective. Few were willing to mess with the things, as there had been too many online videos posted of people who had chosen not to comply—with the results never good for the humans involved.

Other box-shaped droids stood to the sidelines, standing ready behind the dogs. These units looked less intimidating, but Annika knew otherwise; she'd seen them in action. They'd release stun grenades and tear gas into the crowd if the demonstration got out of control. They had been used during similar protests in San Francisco—before the attack.

The ground shook beneath their feet. Calls of surprise and fear broke out as the crowd swayed. A plume of smoke rose from the north, from the direction of Fremont Street.

"What was that?" Becky called above the noise of the surrounding crowd.

"An explosion," Annika replied. "But if you ask where, your guess is as good as mine. We need to keep moving."

Annika looked to the passenger bridge and then to the Strip itself. The bridge would typically be the only way to cross. Giant displays loomed above the stairwell, and without the regular video ads that danced along their surfaces, the behemothic screens felt void of life. Their customary jingles and brash advertising taglines were ominously absent. Even the sound of traffic was gone. The only noise was the roar of protesters echoing off the colossal building that stood next to them. But even that seemed to be muted.

The wall of passengers had spilled onto the street, but only on the fringes. Cars, though inoperative, appeared as if they might start driving again at any moment, as though merely parked in a bout of heavy traffic; a deterrent that, so far, had kept the street mostly clear of pedestrians.

But they had to get to the Grand Kawa, and the only path that made sense to Annika was to cross the street around the evacuated vehicles. Annika eyed the bridge once again. There was no way they'd get through the crowd that mobbed its walkway. Bodies pushed against its glass railing, threatening to dislodge the panes from their fittings and onto the street below.

"Let's just cross here!" she said, grabbing Becky's hand and dropping down the half-foot to street level. Something about diving headfirst into the stationary traffic felt wrong, but there wasn't any alternative.

A green sedan, in the middle of a lane change, blocked their path, its door flung open as its passenger had run off. Navigating around it, they passed another row of vehicles in the far lane, cab-less trucks forming makeshift walls that barricaded them from the west side of the Strip. The autonomous ads-on-wheels required no room for a driver, so the flatbeds simply pressed up against each other.

The drivers of the mobile adverts had been the first to lose their jobs. Unlike rideshare cabs, the moving signs only needed to be programmed in a loop, with no complex destinations necessary. Dozens of them could usually be seen driving the boards up and down the Strip. At first, nobody had really noticed or cared they were gone. The rideshare drivers were next, and it was only after their removal that people began to take notice.

Six of the now motionless boards before them had, at one point, been driving in formation. Computerized synchronization meant they didn't have the same constraints as regular drivers, and their programming was so refined that they had been able to drive less than an inch apart from each other without a problem. The billboards promising showgirls and pool parties clogged the street.

"We're going to have to go around these," Annika said, glancing toward the crowd that was now bulging toward them. "Then we have to somehow find a way inside."

Becky was already positioning herself to avoid the bulk of the crowd. "How are we going to get past this mess?" she asked. "They're all piling toward the entrance!"

"Annika! Becky!" a man's voice called out from the crowd.

Annika tried to ascertain where the voice was coming from, scanning the hordes of people huddled on the sidewalk with nowhere else to go.

A hefty man in an oversized dress shirt stumbled onto the street, headed toward them. It took a moment for Annika to recognize the man was Colby. Part of her was surprised he wasn't waiting for them to show up at the bar in the Paris.

Sweat stained his pale blue dress shirt, his chest sporting damp blotches and circles around his armpits. His shirt had been untucked from his dress pants, and he had lost both the blazer and tie he had been wearing the last time they saw him. A trickle of dried blood was caked to his face, tracing from the top of his forehead and down his left cheek. He looked as though he had been through hell.

"Colby!" Annika yelled. "What happened?"

"I was in a car when they went dark," he huffed as he approached them. "We were just approaching an intersection, and neither car stopped. They collided with each other. But don't worry; it's just a scratch." The back of his arm went to his face and smudged the blood around, mixing with the sweat beading on his forehead.

"You're okay?" Becky asked. "What are you doing here?"

"I'm fine. Tired, but fine. I'm trying to get back to the Kawa," he said, nodding to the golden-windowed building across the street. "I'm guessing that's where you're headed, too? I don't know why I hadn't thought of just crossing the street until I saw you two. They've got us trained to follow the designated path." He looked back at the crowd, practically spilling over the rails. "I'm happy for any excuse not to have to climb those stairs, but I'd much rather be in your company."

Great. Annika thought. *Just what we need.*

"Why are there so many people out here?" Becky asked. "Nobody wanted to stick to their rooms?"

"People are saying the doors of the casinos are locked," Colby said. "Nobody can get in or out."

Annika's gaze climbed the golden tower next to them. Palm trees and replica Japanese architecture blocked her view of the entrance, but the crowd spilling from the walkway up the sidewalk and atop the pedestrian bridge was all she needed to see to confirm what Colby was saying was true.

Cheyenne, she thought. *I have to get to Cheyenne.*

She wouldn't let a locked casino stop her. There had to be another way in.

The ground had been vibrating with the magnitude of people flooding the street, but it now began to shake with more furor. Movement caught Annika's eye, causing her to turn. Behind them, beyond the crowd, machinery crossed the Strip, heading down the Tropicana Highway.

On an average day, it might not have been something she would have noticed from a block and a half away, but with all other vehicles now stationary, their movement was conspicuous. Their electric engines were silent beneath the roars of the crowd, but the rumble of their weight could not be masked.

A hissing from the opposite direction caught her attention, and Annika turned back toward the bridge. She felt the tremor of the earth beneath her feet before she understood what was happening. Smoke and flame burst from the center of the pedestrian bridge as an explosion sent debris rocketing to the sky, tossing dozens of people from above and causing them to burst from the bridge like a popped bag of chips.

"What the hell?" Colby's shout was faint above the screams and the crackle of flames taking hold on the concrete walkway. The three banking administrators instinctively ducked under the advertisement flatbeds beside them, sheltering somewhat from the remnants of raining debris.

Bodies staggered over what remained of the arch, some engulfed in flame, while others pushed their way past the injured, desperate for a reprieve they wouldn't find. Many more slipped and fell over the edge, tumbling to the now smoking concrete below.

Annika froze in the center of the Las Vegas Strip. A concrete block bounced over one car and landed on another only a dozen feet from where she stood. She held her arm out and reflexively turned her face from the impact. Glass burst from the car's windows, and she could feel the movement of the shards as they rushed past her.

She surveyed her blouse and dress pants, carefully brushing away a few stray pieces that had landed on her clothing. In a daze, she realized that what she was doing didn't matter, but she did it anyway, as if glass on her blouse was the biggest of her concerns.

"We need to move." Becky's hand shakily rose above her eyes, trying to block out the sun in order to make sense of what she was seeing. *"Now!"*

Chapter Twelve

Annika

ANNIKA SCRAMBLED to keep up as her friend backtracked behind the six-car train of billboard-clad flatbeds. Becky hardly waited for Annika's response before she sprinted to the last car in the line-up. The woman seemed intent on moving as far away from the blast as possible. Annika couldn't blame her and did her best to catch up.

She couldn't make out what was happening down the street through the smoke, which now billowed over the remnants of the pedestrian bridge, filling the street with its fury. Lights from security bots pierced the haze, along with the screams of people who had just witnessed their friends and neighbors collapsing around them, most likely to their deaths.

Several sedans had stalled against the truck bed in a way that seemed almost intentional, like someone or something hadn't wanted pedestrians to pass by. It made getting to their destination even more arduous, with opened doors and car hoods creating further obstacles to bypassing the chaos. The three colleagues worked their way over and around as quickly as they could manage.

Annika grabbed onto the metal edge of one of the truck beds to hoist herself up and thought there might be just enough room for moving the rest of the way from above. She stood with her back against one billboard promising 'Girls, Girls, Girls' enabling her to gain a new perspective of the assault raging not more than a couple of blocks up the road.

She ascended just in time to witness the next round of hell. More screams erupted as a line of white bots emerged through the settling dust. There were only six of them, but she could feel their weight as bystanders scrambled to escape the flashes of white metal and blue panel lighting. Annika struggled to see their attackers within the mayhem. Their bodies were built top heavy, as though they were meant to emulate bodybuilders or warriors, and flashes of light pulsed from futuristic-looking weapons aimed at the surviving pedestrians, now attempting to flee.

Do those things have ray guns?

Annika was certain these were the same bots that had gone rogue in New York. The images from her eye-piece had gone dark with her cell service, but she could still see the haunting portrait of the video embedded in her mind.

Through the haze, some survivors tried to help others who were trapped beneath the rubble, pushing them forward to escape the next round of terror. The rest were fleeing. Most headed in their direction.

They were in the direct path of the storm, set within the sights of the destructive bots.

Annika's skin crawled. Though their construction was much more intimidating, the similarity of these war machines to Ember was undeniable. The white paneling that covered their bodies, though different in design, was nearly identical in assembly.

Annika was even prepared to bet their humanoid faces were made of the same malleable synthetic skin her own bot possessed. They could easily be the angry cousins of Ember. If *these* bots could go rogue…

She ignored the thought. There was no time to worry about hypotheticals. She had to get to their room, get Cheyenne, and then get somewhere safe. Annika didn't know where that might be, but, at least, it needed to be out of the line of fire until someone came to shut these things down. The police, the military, Batman… Annika didn't care which.

One foot in front of the other, her swollen feet pressed painfully into the ridges of her dress shoes, Annika pushed on, straining against the discomfort.

"Hurry, Colby!" she called back to the manager struggling behind them. They had barely made any ground, and his breath was already labored. He held onto the edge of the billboard truck for support, trying to catch his breath. It was hard to believe that only hours ago, Annika's biggest concern was avoiding having a drink with this man. She'd gladly have several cocktails with the dickwad now if it meant avoiding the reign of terror that surrounded them.

"We can't slow down," she continued. Though she disliked him, she didn't want him to get slaughtered by killer bots either.

"Don't wait for me!" he huffed. "I'll be okay." The man wheezed as he doubled over. He sucked in as much air as he could, waving a hand for them to continue.

Becky, ahead of Annika, hadn't slowed. Colby wasn't going to make it at the rate he was going.

"Get off the street!" Annika called back. "Find cover, at least."

The manager paused, as though giving thought to her suggestion. He looked at the people behind him, and the stampeding crowd appeared to give him new resolve. Colby pushed his way back the way he had come, trying to make it to the sidewalk on the opposite side of the street, making a beeline for a palm tree as though he hoped it might offer him the salvation he craved.

The sound of further gunshots swarmed all around, and Annika recognized conventional gunfire among the distinctive bolts of the bots' ray guns. Annika risked one more glance to see bursts of light being shot from the white beings marching forward.

Red and blue lights flashed behind the bots.

Good, at least the cops are here. Maybe they can get things under control.

"What are you doing?" Becky shouted, circling back around. "We've got to stay ahead of the crowd, or we'll never get inside."

Annika had unconsciously slowed to take a better look at the scene unfolding behind them, but Becky was right; the mob was quickly gaining on them. Even under its current momentum, people were tripping and falling and then being trampled by others trying to flee the same threat. Those desperate to escape the attack would overtake Colby in a matter of seconds.

Flashes of light burst from the bots again. More screams erupted as the panicked crowd scrambled to get out of the way.

A man's voice cried out from across the street, and Annika turned in time to see Colby collapse to the ground, his right hand over his chest. Cries turned to muted garbles, the noise lost in the street's commotion. Colby sprawled over the sidewalk before becoming painfully still.

Annika's heart sank, her mind racing to process what had just happened.

The bots shot Colby. He's dead.

The crowd trampled over the collapsed body as Annika heard herself scream in horror.

She wanted to go after her colleague; to pull him out from

under the stampede. Could she save him? She knew the answer even as she formed the thought. There was no more time to waste.

Annika's feet slapped the pavement, quickly overtaking Becky and maintaining her pace with ease. Annika had never been much of a runner, but pure adrenaline could carry her where she needed to go, and of that, she wasn't in short supply.

Colby's dead.

His head hitting the pavement; his hand over his heart; blood pooling on the street below him as the crowd traipsed over his lifeless body. The scene played in her mind on repeat as they ran.

Annika hadn't liked the man—he was awkward and inappropriate—but she would never have wished death on him. She wouldn't wish a robot uprising on anyone. And yet it seemed she had found herself caught in the middle of one.

And she wasn't with the person who depended on her the most.

Even worse, she had left Cheyenne with a *bot*.

Another couple of blocks ahead, another crowd had gathered in front of a cluster of hotels. Though the crowd was all staring at the plume of smoke now rising into the sky, it didn't appear as if they realized they were in any danger themselves.

Annika wouldn't get close enough to warn them, though. The two friends collectively and silently decided to abandon the main road. They took the first sharp right that presented itself. The road led along the side of the Kawa hotel, toward the parking lot for multiple resorts and the arena. The Las Vegas Knights had played in that arena for forty years, and it still amazed Annika that a city in the middle of the desert was home to an NHL hockey team.

Annika's heart sank as she realized she wouldn't be able

to take Cheyenne to a game. It had been the one thing her sister had wanted to do while in Vegas. There was no way the city would host a game now, even if the rampaging bots were stopped. At best, everything would be shut down for weeks. Admittedly, it was a strange thing to be worried about when their lives were at stake, but Annika's mind flopped around uncontrollably, desperate for something to cling to. Desperate for anything that made sense.

Her brain had yet to fully process the destruction taking place before her eyes. It was like something out of a movie.

A whirring sound overhead caused her to look to the sky in time to witness the arrival of the police drones. The sleek black units hovered over the Strip, zipping frantically from building to building as they assessed the carnage overtaking the streets.

Whatever was happening, Annika thought, it was bigger than a few humanoid bots. It was worse than a few isolated machines out of control; worse than the stray firepower that had killed Colby.

Annika did her best to tune out the weapons fire, to ignore the screams of those who ran by; to ignore the downfall of Las Vegas.

Only a few others had spilled down the back street they were on. The athletic among them had already caught up to the two women, though there were comparatively few. Most of the throng had kept to the Strip. Even down this road, abandoned vehicles stood, clogging the path ahead. Narrow spaces ensured that there wouldn't be many pedestrians who could follow this route in a hurry.

Annika shook her head. Again, the intricate level of obstruction felt as though something or someone had orchestrated the street to be inaccessible, containing the bulk of the crowd to the Strip. Could it all have been planned?

The shock of what had transpired hadn't fully hit her yet.

Annika knew she should be more upset, more scared, more outraged, but only one thing plagued her mind: getting to Cheyenne and getting the hell out of there.

Sparks from drones above unleashed toward the Strip, firing at unseen targets. How the UAVs could target bots without sustaining human casualties was beyond her, but it wasn't her concern at the moment.

Right now, they needed to find a way inside the hotel. Hopefully, something in the back hadn't been locked down, wouldn't be guarded, and would take them far enough away from the robot soldiers that they'd stand a chance, if only a small one.

The bulk of the chaos lay behind them. The few survivors who had followed them along their route had either turned off in other directions or had found somewhere to hide. Becky stopped partway down the block, resting a hand on a vacated blue sedan for a second, before realizing it was too hot to touch. She winced, shaking her hand to cool it down, then moved both hands to her thighs. Sweat streamed down her face, staining the blouse she wore. The late afternoon sun offered no relief.

Annika sucked air as well, putting her hands behind her head and slowing to a walk. She didn't want to stop; they still had so far to go. She eyed the golden tower next to them. Her sister sat waiting for them, forty-eight stories up.

Multi-story parking garages around them sat dark. Annika assumed they would make for great hiding spots if people could get to them. Even without the power outage, they had mostly sat unused for years; a relic from a time when everyone had owned their own vehicles.

Most parking garages had been repurposed or demolished and built over. It was a wonder this one behind the Kawa still stood untouched. It had been excluded from the development of the newer resort and was instead a throwback to a hotel long gone. Annika figured it would likely be remodeled to form part of the connection from the new casino to the shopping centers nearby.

But if they were lucky, the parking garage would be their way in. Since nobody used it, perhaps the bots usually barring entry would have left it unguarded.

She could only hope.

Annika imagined Cheyenne sitting alone in the hotel room. With Ember. Her throat tightened as her heart threatened to leave her chest.

"Becky," Annika said as she slowed her pace. She forced herself to look at her friend instead of the golden towers beside them.

Becky's brown hair hung limp, sweat glistening on her forehead as she hobbled to catch up. Annika hoped that through their exerted effort, the woman hadn't injured herself. Becky inhaled shakily, and she reached out to Annika for support. It was more than just her leg.

"Are you okay?" Annika asked.

They still had stairs to climb. If they were going to make it to her room, an injury wouldn't do them any good, and splitting up wasn't an option Annika wanted to pursue if it could be avoided.

"I'm all right, just tweaked my calf," she replied. "I just need to walk it off a bit."

Annika raised a skeptical eyebrow.

"Seriously," Becky said, "I'm okay. You think we're going to be able to get in this way?" She raised a finger at the parking garage, no doubt hoping to distract Annika.

"I hope so. I can't think of another way to get in. And Cheyenne …" Her words caught in her throat. "Becky, those bots on the road …"

"I know," Becky replied, saving Annika from having to finish her sentence. Becky had come to the same conclusion on her own. "I thought the same thing when I saw the footage from New York. The only other bot I've seen that looks like that is Ember."

"I never wanted that stupid bot!" Annika grabbed fistfuls of her short blonde hair and pulled. "What if … What will I do if …"

She couldn't finish. Ember's design was far too similar to the bots now shooting people and blasting chunks of pedestrian bridges out of the air. Who knew what else they would target? And there was no way of knowing if they'd stop on the street or if their programming would extend to searching the hotels next.

"Are you sure your leg is going to be okay?" she asked Becky. "I'm on the forty-eighth floor and, with the power out, the elevators aren't an option."

And we're going to have to find somewhere safe to run to after.

Annika didn't voice the thought. They had to solve one problem at a time, and there was no point in fatalistic thinking. Once they reached Cheyenne, then they could think about what came next.

Becky took another pensive step, then another, hobbling without putting her full weight on her injured calf.

"Just give me a sec," she said.

Becky did a few stretches and strolled back and forth, muttering to herself, as if giving herself a pep talk.

Annika shot nervous glances down the street. They were running out of time.

"I'm okay." Becky took a full step forward. She seemed to be moving better, but nowhere near as well as she needed to be. The woman's skin was flushed, and her eyes had a slight glaze to them.

Annika's muscles tightened as heavy footsteps approached. What now?

But she breathed a sigh of relief as a man and a woman

appeared, racing out of the parking garage. Both appeared as though they had stepped out of a business meeting and were making a break for it. Obviously, both had spent the day in an air-conditioned hotel, as their attire was far too warm for the desert sun. The man wore a blazer over a t-shirt, blue jeans, and wing-tipped dress shoes, and he was running at a comfortable jogging pace; the woman, a half-step behind him, sported a tan suit and heels that didn't seem to slow her down.

The man turned to her several times, as if to ensure she was keeping up, but from what Annika could tell, she was holding her own.

If Annika was lucky, these two had just escaped through an exit she could use to get inside.

Both were wide-eyed.

"Get out of here!" the man yelled. "You *don't* want to go in there!"

The man slowed, blocking her path. The woman looked up at him tentatively, as if unsure of why he was slowing.

"Do yourselves a favor and get out of here!"

Terre

Terre pulled his arm from Hailey's grasp as she tugged at it, insisting they move on. He couldn't, though; he could see the desperation in the woman who had stumbled into her path. He could see the tears that refused to form and the urgency with which she tugged at her friend. Terre could tell the moment he saw her. It was more than the frenzy of whatever anarchy the bots had unleashed upon the streets; this woman was trying to save someone.

"You don't understand. I have to go inside ..."

Terre gently held up a hand, his palm facing down. "Hold up a sec. What's your name?"

"Annika." Her eyes continued to dart toward the Kawa.

"Well, Annika, unless you've got a death wish, I wouldn't go in there if I were you."

Terre knew they shouldn't stop. The familiar roar of blaster fire, echoing over the chorus of gunshots and blood-curdling screams, confirmed what he already suspected: the bots had taken to the streets of Vegas and were targeting civilians.

As much as he wanted to stick his head in the sand and

wish it all away, Terre knew more were coming. It was going to be San Francisco all over again. It didn't matter whether or not he wanted to be involved; here he was, in the middle of it all once again.

They had a longer journey ahead of them than he cared to admit, and there were thousands of innocent people in the city streets who were going to die. Likely, many already had. Terre was only moving forward, hoping that if they found K, he could prevent more deaths from happening. Terre just hoped it wasn't too late.

Somehow, K was the answer to all of this. A robotics expert didn't just show up in the desert, only miles from the next robot assault, by happenstance.

There was no way to know what the next step would bring, or if it would lead them closer to a solution. Regardless, he had to try, but Terre had no idea how he would get to the dam, and every second mattered.

The blue eyes of the woman before him unwittingly pleaded with him, and something within Terre felt compelled to help.

"You don't want to go into the hotel," he repeated. "We need to run. We've got to get out of here."

The woman shook her head feverishly, tears welling in her eyes but not yet breaking free. "I can't," she said. "I have to go in there."

"There's nothing in there that can't be replaced," Terre said, knowing that it was likely untrue. "If you go in, you might not get back out." He didn't know why he was interfering; the woman could handle her own problems. She certainly didn't need him telling her what to do. But he also didn't want anyone getting hurt if it could avoided. "Bots are malfunctioning, shooting civilians. It's a deathtrap."

"Yeah, I've noticed. They're on the Strip, too. But my

sister's in there," Annika answered. "She's only fourteen, and she's alone in our room."

She looked back to Terre and furrowed her brow, as though just realizing she was spilling her concerns to a total stranger.

"Look, I'm Terre, and this is Hailey. If you go back, it's likely neither you, nor your sister are coming out."

"We need to go, Becky," she said, her eyes now locked onto Terre's. Her lip stiffened as her demeanor shifted to suspicion. "Thanks for the warning."

Though confident, both women looked like hell. Annika was pale, nearly turning green with worry. Makeup, mixed with sweat, ran down her face. Becky appeared in even worse shape, coughing every minute or so, and a limp in her right leg indicated she might have either overexerted herself to reach the Kawa or her muscles were cramping from a lack of fluids. Becky's skin was flushed, her hair matted against her face. A hand frequently lifting to her temple told Terre she had a headache. All signs of dehydration and heatstroke.

Maybe Annika didn't need help, but Becky wouldn't make it anywhere without it.

"What floor's your room on?" Terre asked.

Annika shot him a dirty look. Terre was suddenly aware that the two women knew nothing about him; he was nothing more to them than a strange man who'd stopped them in the street and asked where her solitary teenage sister's room was. He cringed at himself for asking.

"None of your business," Annika snapped. She shot Becky a cautious look. Becky hadn't seemed to notice; she was shielding her eyes from the sun and swaying from the heat.

Terre nodded, unsure of whether to push things further.

The sun reflected off the windows of the golden tower rising above them. This woman's sister was trapped somewhere in there. He couldn't help everyone, but what if he could help *her*? Would it make up for the daughter he couldn't save? Terre pushed down images of the bots attacking while Sarah was happily playing with her toy robots, or whatever her mother would have had her doing at that moment; the moment AI drones launched a strike on their residence and reduced their home to a hole in the ground.

The same images kept him up at night. No matter how many therapy sessions he underwent, the images never changed; never lessened. But each day, he learned how to manage them; learned to live with the horror he had caused. Slowly, Terre was coming to grips with the fact there was nothing he could have done.

How many more parents would be left childless after another attack? How many children would be orphaned? He didn't know Annika or her story, but he knew she was desperate to save a child in danger.

Annika had pushed past him already, and Becky stumbled after her. The woman was going to need hydration and imminent rest, or she'd pass out long before they got anywhere.

"I don't need any help!" Annika asserted as she reached back and grabbed Becky's hand, practically dragging her toward the building. "Thank you, though!"

Terre stared after the pair for a moment. He didn't want to see anyone else lose a family member, but ...

A flash of light from the Strip caught the corner of his eye and ripped him from his thoughts.

"Look out!"

He pushed Hailey to the ground as he leaped toward the two other women, grabbing one in each arm as they all slammed into the pavement below.

A deafening blow struck the parking garage in front of

them. Terre lifted his head in time to watch levels collapsing on top of themselves.

Whatever the machines had fired, it had been more than a simple blaster.

Terre looked back to see Hailey back on her feet, a weapon in hand and pointed at a group of Sentinels. The bots' lights flickered in agitation, their metal unfinished legs quickly closing the gap.

Terre pushed himself up and took a step toward Hailey. As admirable as it was that she was willing to fight back against their attackers, she had no idea what she was up against. Bullets wouldn't even slow them down—their plating was bulletproof. Terre took another step as blue flashes erupted from Hailey's weapon.

She had a blaster. A Cyber Dynamics CD-115, to be precise.

Terre paused. As far as he knew, those weapons weren't available to the public, which meant there was only one place she could have gotten one.

The same place he had.

He had only ever seen those weapons once before—at the Treasure Island US Military Armory, when they were issued to himself and K as they prepared to stop the assault on San Francisco.

The shots missed their marks, but the bots appeared to slow at the new threat. Regardless of the tech Hailey held, however, there were six of them and only one of her.

"Run, you idiots!" she shouted back at them. Seemingly out of nowhere, she grabbed another blaster and tossed it to Terre.

He momentarily fumbled with the CD-115 before gaining control and staring down at it in confusion. With its gray-and-white-paneled covering and a digital interface to adjust its settings, it was identical to the one he had used in San Francisco.

Terre looked blankly at her before he realized she knew exactly what she was doing.

She was giving them time to flee.

Who is this woman?

He considered staying anyway and helping her fend off the bots, but Annika and Becky weren't wasting any time, running for cover toward the hotel. Unarmed, they needed someone to go with them in case more Sentinels showed up.

There was no part of him that wanted to go back inside, especially after seeing the parking garage come crashing down on itself. Even the father within him, crying out to save the child in need, had given pause. But he was no monster. If San Francisco was any template for what was about to occur, this wouldn't end well, and the girl waiting inside the building could use all the help she could get.

Without a word, Terre gave Hailey a parting glance and hurried to catch up. Annika and Becky were nearly at the hidden entrance and were going to dart right past it.

"Get out of the city, Hoffman!" Hailey called over the roar of blaster fire. "And make sure you find Kristopher!"

Terre stopped and nearly choked. He was sure he hadn't told her his surname, or Kristopher's name, and it was doubtful he would have uttered his full name, instead preferring the nickname 'K.' He had to fight every urge within him to not turn around, grab Hailey, and interrogate her about how she knew about the man Fredricks had instructed him to find.

But there was no time, and he'd likely kill them both.

"Annika!" he called. "There's an entrance here." He pointed to the landing he and Hailey had emerged from. A sole metal ladder attached to the side of a makeshift wall led up to the plastic lining that fringed the construction site.

Annika slowed and gave her friend a suspicious look. The second woman seemed to have barely noticed they had stopped running, let alone had the fortitude to offer an opinion about the stranger they had just encountered.

Terre couldn't say he blamed Annika for having doubts about him, but they didn't have the time or luxury of being cautious.

"Those bots aren't going to just wait for us," he insisted. "This is how I got out of the building. It will get us back in."

The second woman was doubled over, dry heaving into a palm-leafed bush in a cement planter beside the building.

Annika put a hand on her friend's back and the woman straightened, her face as pale as a Sentinel.

"You going to be okay, Becky?" she asked.

Becky nodded unconvincingly and wobbled as she attempted to put one foot in front of the other.

And he was going to make her climb a ladder.

"She's not okay," Terre said. "We need to get her inside, out of the sun, or she won't make it."

"What's it to you?" Annika's eyes blazed ice as she focused on him.

"Look, I'm just trying to help. Your friend's severely dehydrated. We need to get her out of the heat and get some fluids into her."

"Why do you care?" she asked again, the edge to her words lifting slightly and one eyebrow arched as she guided Becky to the edge of the ladder.

Terre took a deep breath. Why *did* he care? She was one woman among thousands who probably wouldn't survive the next twenty-four hours, unless he found K. And that was assuming K held the answer.

If he expected the women to trust him, he had to lay all his cards on the table.

Terre sighed, keeping one eye on the battle between the

Sentinels and the mysterious woman who had chatted with him at the bar. Hailey had somehow led the bots further down a side street, away from them. With the dust and debris in the air, he couldn't make out much more than the occasional blue beam of blaster fire. Hailey had bought them a few moments, but he knew the reprieve wouldn't last long.

"The bots killed my wife and daughter." He shook his head, wondering how much of it mattered. Had their deaths been in vain? Saving this woman's sister wouldn't change anything. "Look, you're obviously capable women. You don't need me tagging along, trying to be the hero. Just make sure she gets some water. I have someone else I need to find."

Perhaps it wasn't too late to go back for Hailey, not that she needed his help, either.

Annika took one look at Becky and another at the ladder leading up the side of the wall. Her gaze extended upward, and Terre feared how many floors up her sister was. The sound of blaster fire grew louder around the corner they came from. Terre couldn't help but wonder how Hailey was doing.

Annika sighed as she seemed to realize the severity of her friend's situation. "I probably could use some help." It looked like she wanted to say more, but she swayed and put a hand against the side of the building.

"Are *you* able to climb?" Terre asked.

Annika took another deep breath, stabilizing herself, and nodded. "I'm okay. It's Becky I'm worried about. Will you be able to help me get her up?"

"Sure."

"Climb up. You can pull while I push."

Terre jumped up the ladder, conscious that the noise from the street was growing louder. If the Sentinels pursued them into the building, there would be no way to outrun them. He had to help get the women inside before that could happen.

Annika led Becky to the ladder and helped to position her hands on the rungs. Becky stood staring at her hand, tears welling in her eyes.

"Come on, Becky!" Terre shouted. "You can do this."

Becky lifted her eyes in a daze, her forehead wrinkled and her eyes blank, as though she had no recollection of who Terre was or why he was encouraging her to climb the emergency ladder.

But then, in a moment of clarity, the fog lifted, and her face relaxed. Becky reached up for the next rung on the ladder, and then the next. Annika stood below her, encouraging her the entire way with bouts of "Good job, Becky!" and "Almost there!"

Terre reached down, grabbed one of Becky's cold hands, and helped her onto the landing. The sweat on his own arm emphasized how dry hers was.

Blaster fire and the lit panels of the Sentinels shone through the settling dust as they rounded the corner of the adjacent building.

Hailey came running from within the cloud.

"What are you *still* doing out here!" she yelled in between shots. "Don't let them see you!"

Robotic eyes glowed at the edge of the building. Terre didn't know how much or how far the bots could see. It might already have been too late.

But he jumped anyway, pulling Becky with him. Annika stumbled behind as they slipped through the plastic curtain and into the shadows.

Chapter Fourteen

Terre

TERRE CONTINUED to glance over his shoulder as they raced down the hallway, back into the construction zone he had just escaped. Three things plagued his mind: finding water for the women he had just met; the Sentinels on their tail; and who the hell Hailey really was.

Signs were pointing to Hailey being a CIA agent, or at least someone connected to Fredricks. There was no other way to explain her knowledge of K or her proficiency with the CD-115 she had in her possession.

She knew *exactly* what she was doing, the ill-preparedness she had dramatized little more than a smokescreen.

Terre held up his phone and used its flashlight to navigate through the darkened cavern. He hated to waste his battery, but the emergency lights weren't cutting it, and they couldn't risk an injury tripping over a cord or a wayward scrap of metal. The maintenance bots had all fled, but there was still construction material placed in piles, and though the bots had been fairly neat in their operations, he didn't want to take any chances.

The noise coming from the casino had increased in the

short time he had been outside. The fake wall had managed to keep people out, but the roar of the crowd had amplified. Their dissent must have been moving closer.

Annika and Becky appeared to be moving a little better now that they were out of the sun, but it was tough to tell if it would be enough.

Terre moved in close enough to Annika so that she'd be able to hear him without raising his voice. "How long had you been out there?" he asked. "Where were you coming from?"

"We were at the Convention Center," Annika answered. The grit in her voice told Terre this wasn't the first time she'd been in an emergency, as though she was tackling the situation with an underlying bitterness. Finding her sister was only part of what was going through her head. Terre guessed that the woman had already lost someone close to her. The resolve not to lose her sister was palpable, practically burning hot on her skin.

"We'd just finished for the day when the power went out. We had to walk back."

That had been a couple of hours ago; enough time to be concerned if they weren't used to the desert heat.

"What room are you in?" Terre asked, trying his luck again. "We're going to need to take the stairs. The elevators are down."

Terre could tell Annika was doing her best not to react to the news. Her hand trembled slightly as she brought it up to her forehead. She pretended to brush the hair from her eyes as she noticed the involuntary motion.

"Forty-eight oh-oh-two," she said with a deadpan expression.

Terre sighed. He had been afraid of that. He'd have no problem making the climb, and Annika could probably manage, but it was going to be a stretch for Becky. Hopefully, they'd make it to the room and back before the orbs raged overhead.

The entrance to the casino stood before them. A few quick turns would lead them onto the main floor. Agitated chatter and loud, booming outrage from the other side of the makeshift wall betrayed that tensions were continuing to rise and patience was running thin.

"All right," Terre said. "Once we get onto the casino floor, if you follow this temporary wall to your left, it will take you to a stairwell. You and Becky make your way up to your room. I'm going to find some water. I'll catch up with you."

Annika's blue eyes grew wide, the whites reflecting in the harsh light of Terre's phone.

"You're going to leave us, aren't you?" It wasn't an accusation as much as it was a statement. Annika's voice betrayed no emotion; she could have been telling him to grab a coffee.

Terre started at the question. The thought hadn't even crossed his mind. Hardly fifteen minutes had passed since this woman had essentially told him to take a hike, and now she was concerned he was going to abandon them?

Terre turned off his phone's light, leaving them with the glow of the casino lights streaming over the wall.

Images of Cara had plagued his mind for months. In those visions, she asked him why he'd left them; why he'd let them die. Shapes in the darkness played games with his vision. He reached to the wall for support as his dead daughter's face confronted him. The hallucinations were as real and as solid as the horrific nightmares that wreaked havoc in his sleep.

Terre realized he had dimmed the light as much to hide the emotion in his own eyes, but he couldn't disguise the quiver in his voice. He rarely cried, though lately he had been waking to a wet pillow and streaks down his face.

The light from the casino was sufficient for him to make

out Annika's features. Her short blonde hair framed her slender face, and her streaked makeup gave her an appearance of being destitute, but Terre could tell she was anything but. Her shoulders were back and her head was held high, despite the mounting pressure weighing her down.

"I wouldn't dream of it," he said. "I promise."

Had he promised Sarah the same thing? Flashbacks of the attack muddled his memory of the interaction with his daughter that morning. The assault had knocked him unconscious, and he had nearly died himself. He hadn't known then that disaster had been imminent, but he had promised to fix the sensors. What other promises had he made to her that were now left unfulfilled?

"I'd love to tell you to take your time," Terre said, "but we need to get your sister and get out of here. The clock's ticking."

"Why?" Becky paused, her brow piquing as she tilted her tired head. "What's happening?" She was becoming more alert, which was good, but they didn't have time to go into explanations. If Onyx drones appeared to assist the Sentinels, the top floor of a heavily populated building was the last place they wanted to be.

"I'll explain once I catch up," he said. "Make a start on those stairs. I'll be there soon."

Terre noticed Becky's lips narrow as she passed. Terre could understand her not wanting to be left in the dark, but they couldn't afford to waste more time. They were already pushing their luck.

"If you're going to help us," Annika said in a hushed tone so Becky couldn't hear, "hurry back. If you're just going to abandon us, let me know now."

"I won't do that," he said. "I promise. But Becky's not going to get very far unless we get her some water. Go to your sister. I'll meet you there. Forty-eight oh-oh-two."

Terre didn't wait for a response. He patted his newly acquired CD-115 in his belt as an unconscious reassurance. The mass of people had indeed made their way deeper into the casino, but they had yet to discover the hidden entry through the construction zone.

It had now been several hours since the power had gone out. Terre surveyed the golden carpet, watching for an obvious path to follow among the people sitting huddled on the floor, or an easy access vendor to grab a few waters from. The crowd was audibly disgruntled, but, so far, it didn't seem to be anything Security couldn't handle. Every barstool at the Sakana Tamago bar was now filled with over-indulged faces. Standing patrons peeked between those who sat. Some were leaning on those fortunate enough to have a seat.

As long as they remain happy drunks, Terre thought, though he wondered how long that illusion would last.

The bar triggered thoughts of Hailey. He wondered if she'd made it, and if he'd see her again. She'd made it clear they were to leave the city, echoing Fredricks's request. She'd put herself in jeopardy so he could escape with Annika and Becky. It was clear to him now that she had been there with a purpose. She hadn't met or followed him by accident, and something told him he hadn't seen the last of her.

Typically flagging down an automated cart would have been the quickest way to order, but nearly every person currently had a drink in their hand or was waiting for one and the mechanized staff couldn't keep up. Not that a human crew would have fared any better.

A small convenience store sat hidden in an outlet. Tacky souvenirs, t-shirts, and magazines offered waning moments of distraction for those trying to kill a few moments away from the casino. Right now, though, nobody was too concerned with the trinkets that hung from its shelves. A few mothers brought their children through the store, keeping them entertained for a few moments with the promise of a candy bar or the latest comic book.

As with everything else at the Kawa, the convenience store was completely automated. He grabbed a backpack off the rack and loaded it with bottles of water and sports drinks, as well as a few protein bars and other packets of snacks. The stairs were one thing; if he was going to head out into the desert, he didn't want to leave unprepared.

Terre shook his head as he swiped his resort pass over the reader to charge his purchases to his room. He didn't even look at the price; it didn't matter what the damage would be. Fredricks had better be reimbursing him for this entire endeavor.

Screams from the casino floor stopped Terre cold in his tracks.

His time was up.

He heaved the bag onto his back. It was heavier than he had intended, but he wasn't about to readjust for weight now.

Above the cries, blaster fire and shattering glass resonated. Terre turned the corner in time to see the white hard-bodied Sentinels jumping over tables, blasters in hand. He could only surmise what that meant for the people who remained on the street.

There were at least six bots Terre could see firing indiscriminately into the crowd. Cries followed those running for their lives to the back of the casino, now their only option.

They were all headed right for Terre.

He would have loved to have stood his ground and take his blaster to help those rushing toward him, but he'd be of no use to Annika and Becky if he died in a heroic fight. He'd be no match against six Sentinels on his own, nor for the stampede they'd started.

The security guard who had helped Terre earlier stood in

front of the blackjack tables. He lifted a handgun and fired three shots before blaster rays struck him in the chest, sending him flying across the table. Fits of screams intensified around him as fleeing guests tripped over themselves trying to get away. Further into the casino, Terre could make out bodies going down. Blaster fire lit up the floor, sending blue beams into the flesh of the ensnared hotel patrons.

Terre didn't waste any time watching the aftermath. The bots weren't slowing in their assault, and he guessed their programming mandated the elimination of anyone who stood in their way.

The mob had yet to reach his location, and so Terre did his best to hug the wall back to the entrance of the staircase. His guess was that people fleeing the casino wouldn't choose to go up flights of stairs, but then again, those who were desperate might take the first path they came across to get to perceived safety.

His watch ticked violently against his wrist, as if he needed reminding that time was running short. If Fredricks was right, a few Sentinels was going to be the least of his problems.

Blaster fire lit up the dark recesses behind the half-wall of the construction site. The bots Hailey had been chasing must have found their point of entry.

The Kawa was surrounded.

Terre swallowed as he wondered what that meant for Hailey, but he didn't have time to dwell on what might have happened to the woman. For the moment, he needed to worry about how to get to Annika and Becky and then figure out a way to get back outside.

He inhaled sharply; now that the bots had breached the inside of the hotel, he didn't know how that was going to be possible.

His hand rested on his shirt, where the CD-115 Hailey had tossed to him was still concealed. Maybe it was foolish of him not to have it drawn, but he wanted to have his hands free, just in case he needed to use them quickly.

Gunfire rang through the facility, louder than anything else among the chaos. It made the blaster fire sound impotent in comparison, but Terre knew it would have little effect on the bulletproof-plated machines.

Bullets would only be effective if enough of them struck the fleshy head of the Sentinels, but a few gouges to their synthetic skin didn't appear to slow them down; it just made them more grotesque. Metal skulls with circuitry, wires hanging out, bits of fake skin and muscle hanging in strips.

The shooters behind the tactical weapons didn't seem to have the skill to hit their target. Terre was sure there were many highly capable marksmen in the crowd, but he had seen the Sentinels' schematics; the military had built the machines to anticipate attacks, to detect what was coming at them faster than the human mind could perceive. He was sure they could see the bullets coming and calculate repositioning before impact.

Terre instinctively ducked as he ran, though it likely slowed him down. He followed the wall, not wanting to be pushed further away from the stairwell than he needed to be. At the speed Becky had been moving, the two women probably hadn't made it much further than a dozen floors, maybe two.

At the end of a small hall, the door to the stairs sat quiet and unassuming; a beacon of hope set apart from the terror that waged on behind him.

Terre yanked the door open just enough to allow his body and the pack he wore to squeeze through. He pulled the door shut behind him and locked it, looking around frantically for a stick or a bar of some sort to shove through the handles, but there was nothing suitable nearby.

The lock would only temporarily slow the crowd—until they became desperate.

Terre swallowed the guilt at leaving so many people on the casino floor to die, but he knew, realistically, there was little he could do. Filling the stairwell with a few hundred frightened people would only briefly delay their deaths—and assure his.

Locking the door also assured Hailey couldn't follow him, and he felt guilty about leaving her behind, even though she seemed to be more than capable of holding her own. Her knowledge of the mission made it a safe bet Fredricks had sent her to ensure he got the job done. Terre had no real reason to believe she'd try to come back inside the Kawa.

He shook his head as he lifted a foot to climb the first of what would be hundreds of stairs. Despite everything he had been through in the past few weeks, this was still surreal.

Hailey had appeared far more trained for combat than he could ever dream of being. She knew how to fire a weapon, and how to draw the fire of those bots and distract them well enough for him to escape with Annika and Becky.

His hand rested unconsciously on his CD-115. He barely knew how to fire it, never mind be proficient enough to do an adequate job of defense. It would be a last-ditch effort, and he prayed he didn't have to find out just how badly it would go.

He pushed his thoughts aside, doing his best to ignore the screams and gunfire coming from the other side of the stairwell door. For now, all he could do was focus on the climb ahead.

Chapter Fifteen

Annika

HE'S LEFT *us to die.*

Annika's thoughts darkened as she collapsed on the landing in the stairwell. She had lost count of how many floors they had ascended, and it was too disheartening to read the numbers.

They had started off well, but after ten floors, the heat exhaustion had kicked in and Becky had needed to use the rail to push herself along up the next few levels. Annika did her best to encourage the woman, even giving Becky her shoulder to take some of her weight. But by the twentieth floor, Annika's limbs had started to shake and give out as well, and she could no longer provide Becky with any support.

Somehow, they had managed to crawl up an additional three, maybe four, floors, but they were barely halfway to their destination.

With each step, Annika thought of a new curse to prod herself along. She felt ridiculous and panicked at the same time. Climbing a few flights of stairs shouldn't be so difficult —she didn't care how dehydrated she was.

Cheyenne's counting on me.

Annika took a deep breath, allowing her lungs to fill with the warm, stale air of the stairwell.

I just need to rest. Then I'll keep going.

Annika slid to the floor. Becky was still a floor behind, so she'd allow her friend to catch up. The concrete cooled her body as she pressed herself against it.

Terre should be here by now. He's bailed on us.

The man had saved their lives, and so had the woman he was with, Hailey. In fact, she had seemingly sacrificed herself so the three of them could retreat into the Kawa. But Terre had left Hailey alone to fight those robots on her own. She had tossed him a ray gun, but instead of helping her hold off the bots, he had bailed to save his own skin. And now he had likely done the same thing to her and Becky.

It didn't matter. She was here to save Cheyenne. Terre owed them nothing. Another empty promise wasn't about to stop her from saving her sister.

Annika lifted her head just enough to see her friend sprawled, face first, on the floor next to her. Becky had caught up and then proceeded to collapse, her torso rising and falling the only indication she was still alive. She needed to let Becky rest. If by some miracle Terre was still on his way, he'd catch up to them. If not, they'd perhaps pull together enough strength to carry on.

Annika knew Becky needed more aid than a quick stop on the stairs though, and Becky would need to pull herself together long enough for them to escape the Strip, and that was if the bots weren't terrorizing the rest of the city.

They both would.

Annika shook her head and pushed herself up into a sitting position, letting her back rest against the concrete wall. Cheyenne was her priority. If she accomplished nothing else, it would be to get her sister safely out of the city.

She shook her head. Hours ago, she had been giving a lecture on how robots wouldn't take their jobs, and now she was fleeing ones that were trying to shoot at her. It seemed jobs were the least of their worries.

If she had stayed in Saskatchewan, Annika could have watched all of this on the news, rather than living it. Events seemed so far away when watching them unfold online.

And yet, Annika knew she had been lucky. So far. She shuddered to think of the people on the Strip and what they were going through—*if* any of them were still alive. Annika had only had a small taste of the destruction. Hailey had suffered the brunt of that attack.

For some reason, she had believed Terre and Hailey would have provided them with a way out of the city. Now, it appeared she and Becky were on their own. They could barely function, never mind pull off a rescue

And then what? Wander into the Nevada desert? It was clear vehicles were out of the question. Marlene and Darla were probably dead now, blown to pieces on their way to the pool.

Colby was also dead. He might have been obnoxious, but he hadn't deserved to die.

She felt the rise and fall of her abdomen as she centered herself, calling on whatever reserve strength she had left from protecting and taking care of Cheyenne for the past seven years. Cheyenne had already survived so much, and both of them had lost more than their fair share to artificial intelligence, including their parents.

Annika wasn't going to let them take Cheyenne as well. She had to continue.

"Becky," she said, shaking her friend gently. "I need to keep going."

Becky groaned and rolled over. She opened her eyes,

glossy and distant, and stared at the ceiling as she answered softly, "Okay."

Annika looked up the stairwell. So far, they had encountered nobody else, which was surprising with the elevators out of order, and she wondered how long it would be until people became more desperate to leave their rooms.

There was no point in forcing Becky to continue. Annika refused to abandon her friend but allowing her to rest would be the best thing for her.

I'll be back. I promise.

"You stay here," she said. "If Terre doesn't catch up to you first, I'll bring water down for you and something from our room. If Cheyenne hasn't eaten all the snacks."

She had meant it as a joke, but she wiped the smile from her face when her friend didn't react. Becky simply blinked and nodded. "*Mmm-hmm,*" she murmured, and closed her eyes.

A moment of panic overtook her. Becky appeared as if she might be past the point of water and snacks. She was going to need rest—a lot of it.

Becky's clammy hand grabbed Annika's arm, preventing her from standing. "Please don't leave me," Becky managed, her eyes still unfocused as she slurred her words. "I don't want those things to get me."

Annika took another deep breath.

"I have to get Cheyenne," Annika replied, gripping Becky's hand. She squeezed, and Becky's grip on her arm relaxed. "Once I have her, I'll come back for you. We'll all leave together."

Becky didn't look convinced; her pale face just stared up at her in horror. Annika could tell Becky didn't believe she'd return; that she'd leave her alone—just like Terre had.

"I promise. You need to rest, and I can't carry you up the stairs. But I also can't sit and wait, either. Please, Becks. I'll come back with Cheyenne, you'll have had some rest, and then we can get out of here."

"I don't want to be left alone." A single tear had formed and streamed down Becky's face, trailing down her cheek and leaving a trail of dirt behind. Annika hadn't realized how dirty they'd both become from running through the dusty streets of Vegas. She wiped a sweaty backhand over her forehead and looked at the smudge of black on her arm as she pulled it away.

"We both can't stay here," Annika insisted. "I have to get Cheyenne. I'll be back soon."

Tears left tracks down Becky's cheeks, and Annika felt more relief than regret. If she could form tears, it meant she hadn't completely succumbed to heatstroke yet. Rest would definitely be the best thing for her.

Annika shook off Becky's arm as she stood, her legs wobbly beneath her but still reliable. She was tired, her legs ached, and her back was screaming at her, but the alternative was worse. If she waited any longer, she wouldn't be able to muster enough energy to go.

"What do I do if the bots come?" Becky asked, her arm falling slack as she reluctantly let go of Annika's. "I don't want to die."

"If you hear anything coming up those stairs, then find somewhere to hide. Head through this door and find a room. I think we have some time, though."

Annika had no way of knowing if that was true or not, but if she could help ease Becky's mind, even temporarily, it was worth it.

Before Becky could say anything else to talk her out of it, Annika took a few steps toward the next floor. Her legs were like jelly, wobbling beneath her, threatening to buckle, but she couldn't give up now.

One step at a time. Just one more step.

As she continued, the strength seemed to return miraculously to her legs. New life found her as Annika focused on her goal. If she didn't have the strength to do it for herself or for Becky, she would find it for Cheyenne. She had made a promise, and she intended to keep it.

I'm strong. I'm capable. I will *help Cheyenne.*

The mantra encouraged her, and Annika managed to increase her momentum, her strength returning until she was nearly skipping steps on the way up. She consciously slowed her own movements, afraid of overexerting herself on pure adrenaline.

Before she knew it, she was passing floor forty.

Vigor coursed through her veins. Annika wondered if she'd have enough time for a shower when she got to the room. She shook off the thought; there was no time. They had to get out of the building. Terre had no reason to lie about that. It was likely what he had done. He had seemed hesitant to re-enter the hotel in the first place.

There was no time for anything except for her to grab Cheyenne, perhaps a bag of basic items, and head out.

Dizziness threatened to overtake her once again as Annika remembered one other piece of the puzzle she had pushed to the back of her mind.

Ember.

The Keeper bot was with Cheyenne, and with everything else going on with the tech in the city, Annika had no way of knowing how it would behave.

The AI-driven cars had stopped but had locked their passengers inside. Some of the security and police bots appeared to have turned on the citizens they had been programmed to protect, but not all. Would Ember be any different?

Annika cursed under her breath for the hundredth time that afternoon. She had potentially left her sister in the care of a homicidal computer. She'd never forgive herself if she lost another family member to AI.

After the fire had raged through their farm and their parents had disappeared, Annika hadn't known what she was going to do. She had barely completed high school, and her job prospects had been slim. Adding in a younger sister who needed a guardian was an additional strain to her life, but Annika had sworn she'd do anything to keep Cheyenne with her and out of foster care. When the Canadian government had offered victims of climate disasters the assistance of the Keeper bots, she'd barely hesitated to apply. As much as she hated the tech, she needed to keep what was left of her family together more.

Any job she had been qualified for had been automated away. Annika had planned to go to a trade school and had been trying to decide what program to apply for when the fire hit. It wouldn't have made a difference, anyway. Even with certification or a diploma, there were more bodies than spots to fill.

Her saving grace had been small-town generosity. The Regional Manager of their Credit Union happened to have been a friend of her father. He'd offered her a position, despite a mile-high pile of applications. Once she was in, Annika had worked hard to earn her role and be the best she could be at it. It was how she came to be giving a presentation to others in her position at only twenty-five. She was easily one of the youngest people in that session, and she was the person *presenting* it.

Annika took a deep breath as floor forty-one passed her by. She was almost there.

Her legs still felt strong. She was certainly dehydrated, but her spirits had lifted. There wasn't much further to go. She was going to make it to the forty-eighth floor.

She rounded the corner to the platform of floor forty-two and found herself staring down the barrel of a shotgun.

"Well, hello, gorgeous."

Chapter Sixteen

Annika

A TOXIC SCENT COMBINING VANILLA, caramel, and the hot sourness of alcohol filled Annika's senses. Smells that, individually, could have been soothing if they resulted from a nice hot bath. The combination was wrong—she'd had enough roughneck uncles to know it as the stench of cheap bourbon. Her stomach roiled even before she got a good look at the man who stood on the platform above her.

The man holding the shotgun wore ripped, loose-fitting jeans and a pair of steel toe cap boots. Dirty blond hair had been tucked under a ball cap, and three-day-old stubble covered the man's face.

She instinctively put her hands up. There were many hunters in her community of Saskatoon, so she was no stranger to being around guns, but she had never had one pointed at her. The only time she had wielded a weapon herself was to scare coyotes away from their chickens, and her aim hadn't needed to be very good to do that.

"Don't shoot!" The sound of her pulse, already quickened from the march up the stairs, was heavy in her ears.

The man took a hand off his weapon to scratch his

stomach, wrinkling his white t-shirt. He then adjusted his ball cap, tilting it to the side with two fingers on the brim, as though it were obstructing his view.

"You look like hell," he said.

Coming from you, I must be on death's door, she thought.

"I'm just trying to get back to my room," she said. Her heart raced; she had nowhere to run, and nobody to come to her rescue.

"You're all alone?" the man said, echoing her thoughts. His words were slurred enough to reveal he'd indulged in more than one of those bourbons.

Annika recognized the glint in his eye and knew the gun might be the least of her worries. The weapon shook unsteadily in his hand, and Annika worried he might fire it by mistake.

"No …" she said, as convincingly as she could, crossing her arms in front of her. "My boyfriend stopped to get us water. He'll be up soon."

The man looked past Annika, as if expecting someone to be right on her heels. She prayed to any deity that would listen for Terre to mosey up in that instant, but with a shotgun pointed in their direction, she doubted there was anything he'd be able to do.

"We're forty-two floors up, and he hasn't caught up to you yet. Honey, I don't think he's coming back."

Her heart sank at the truth in his statement. Somehow, the man had seen through her bluff and into her nightmares. She'd been abandoned. All afternoon, she'd feared she would die at the hands of the bots, just like her parents, but it turned out some drunk guy on the forty-second floor of the Kawa Grand Hotel might beat them to it instead.

Suddenly, death by robot didn't seem like such a cruel fate.

"He just stopped off to look for a vending machine," Annika replied, desperately trying to sound confident.

"Well, maybe we can have our own fun before he gets back?" The glint in the man's eyes turned dangerous as they hardened and the smile on his face flattened.

Annika realized then nothing would deter this guy; not the threat of a boyfriend, and definitely not a polite "no." A knee to the groin would be on the table if she could get close enough, but the gun to her head made it all but impossible.

"I'm good, thanks," she said. Annika reflexively took a step back. Her mind raced for a way to get out. There'd be no going past him, and she didn't think she could move fast enough down the stairwell, either.

He cocked the hammer on his gun, removing all doubt. "I think you should come with me."

Annika froze. She was half a flight of stairs and seven feet away. Maybe she could fall back and hope she could lose him on the way down, but it was too risky a move with a gun pointed at her face and an unsteady drunk on the trigger.

It wasn't her own safety she was concerned about; she needed to keep Cheyenne in mind. She couldn't help her sister with buckshot in her chest.

"Hey now!" she said, trying to maintain her composure. "There's no need for that."

"Let *me* decide what there's a need for," he growled. "I'm going to show you a good time. Don't try anything stupid. Come here, one step at a time. Keep your hands up, right where they are."

When she didn't move, the man lifted the gun and fired at the ceiling. Clanging metal and failing debris forced her to duck.

"You need to work on your listening skills," he said. He didn't raise his voice, but his calm determination made it clear he wouldn't tolerate anything but compliance. "I said come here."

"Okay." Annika's voice trembled. If this man was crazy enough to discharge his shotgun in a stairwell, there was no telling what else he might do. "Just don't shoot again." She took a step, slow and controlled, doing her best to hide the waver in her limbs.

"That's more like it. Now, don't try anything stupid."

But only stupid scenarios were going through her head. It was clear he wouldn't hesitate to shoot her. There wasn't a way out that she could see. If she tried to gain the upper hand or attempted to flee down the stairs, there was a good chance he would pull the trigger.

But if she followed him to his room, there might be a fate worse than death within those walls.

Especially if more of his friends were waiting in the room for him.

Surely there were security cameras on this floor? She imagined they'd run on backup power for more than a few hours. Would security bots come? Or were they otherwise engaged?

"The power hasn't been out for *that* long," she said, as calmly as she could muster. "Surely you don't want to resort to kidnapping and murder already?"

"This isn't about kidnapping," he said, shotgun waving wildly as he flapped his hands about. "This is about having a good time and enjoying the end."

Before she could blink, he reached down, grabbed her arm, and pulled her up the last few steps. He moved remarkably fast for someone barely able to speak straight.

"They want to replace us all with robots. Don't want any of us to have jobs or have fun. Well, we'll show them, won't we, gorgeous? We'll show them who can have a good time."

His fingers dug into Annika's arm, pinching the muscles

so tightly that she swore he'd bruise her. She thought about granting her attacker a swift kick to the shin or a jab to the stomach, but he pressed the cold metal of his weapon to the back of her head and immediately quelled any thoughts she had of retaliation.

"Is the gun really necessary?" she asked. "It'll be hard for us to have a good time with that in the way."

"Oh, you think I'm pretty stupid, don't you?" he said. "I know your type. Would rather fight me. I bet you'd rather give your life over to one of them machines? Let them do everything for you? Well, not me! I won't let them do that to me!"

The drunk wasn't making any sense, and she realized she wouldn't make any headway trying to reason with him. She would be okay with being shot in the head over whatever other perverted plan he had for her, but Cheyenne was still upstairs, and, if nothing else, she needed to get to her sister.

The man slapped something on her wrist, and she jumped as it pinched her flesh. At first, she thought he'd slit her wrists, but as he lowered the weapon from her cranium, she tugged her arms and realized he had slapped handcuffs on her.

The act confused her more than caused fear—she'd take handcuffs over a gun to her temple any day. But who was sitting around in their hotel room with handcuffs and a shotgun, waiting for the power to go out?

She swore under her breath.

This guy really is a pervert.

She had ended up at the wrong place at the wrong time.

"What were you doing in the stairwell?" she asked. Perhaps she could learn something or distract him enough to flee. "Doesn't seem like the best place to meet women."

The man scoffed. "This," he waved with his free hand, "the power outage, the bot malfunctions ... Have you had a look outside? It's *chaos*. The boss sent us here for a purpose, and just in the nick of time. You think this wasn't planned? San Francisco was just a trial run. We're going to show them all that they can't use bots to control us."

Annika felt her face contort as she tried to decipher what the man was trying to say.

"You didn't answer my question." Annika did her best to slow their pace; she didn't want to enter the room and face whatever sick plans the man had formed. If she could keep him in the hall for as long as possible, perhaps she'd have a chance. Perhaps somebody would step out of their room and come to her rescue. Her limbs felt like jelly—not from the climb, and not from heat exhaustion, which was still a real threat—and fear coursed through her veins, weighing her down, sending what little adrenaline her body had in reserve through her.

"I'm keeping watch," he said. "I was expecting the bots, but I found you instead. A blonde angel instead of a metal demon. It's a sign we're doin' the right thing."

"I don't understand," she said.

"You will, gorgeous. I'll take care of us. The bots will never take control. We'll show 'em."

Annika wrinkled her nose, but the man didn't offer any further information. What exactly was he planning? Was this the ramblings of a drunk, or was there something else behind his words?

"My boyfriend's going to be pissed," she said. She had to try something. "He's a UFC fighter, by the way. You're going to be sorry."

"I'm not worried about some brute. He won't be here much longer. They'll all pay for letting humanity come to this. Then it'll just be us. Us, and others like us. They'll see. We'll rebuild the world in our image."

The man continued to mutter unintelligibly to himself.

Annika decided it was best if she didn't press him to talk more. He was clearly inebriated past the point of making any sense.

The hall was long and winding, as most within Las Vegas hotels tended to be. She didn't have to fake stumbling and tripping over her feet several times. Emergency lighting provided enough luminescence to make out the red carpeting and paintings composed by various Asian artists that lined the hall. Chills went down her spine. Trapped in what was essentially a dungeon forty-two stories in the sky, she needed to find a way to escape—and soon.

The man fumbled in his pocket before pulling out a keycard and waving it in front of the reader. It beeped and flashed green before he pushed down the handle.

The door opened, and Annika held back a gasp as she realized the situation that awaited her was much worse than she could ever have imagined.

Chapter Seventeen

Terre

TERRE STAYED quiet in the stairwell as the stranger held Annika at gunpoint. There wasn't anything he'd could do until he could get in a better position. Shooting up a stairwell would put him at a serious disadvantage, especially with next to no weapons experience and with Annika in between her assailant and him.

So instead, Terre crouched around the corner and waited.

No margin for error, my ass, he thought, reflecting on his earlier conversation with the security guard.

Whether the AI-operated security system was down or simply preoccupied with the assault happening in the casino, it somehow hadn't picked up on the armed psychopath sitting in the stairwell.

He had left most of his supplies with Becky, assuming he'd be coming right back down with Annika and her sister. Becky had greedily drunk from the water and Terre had had to slow her down so she didn't get sick. He'd given her one of the sports drinks he'd grabbed from the convenience store and told her to sip it until he got back. She needed the electrolytes.

"You'll start to feel better by the time we get back," he'd said.

He only hoped it was true. Though the two women had made it further than he had expected in the short amount of time they were apart, Becky was moving from moderate exhaustion to something more concerning. Becky had stopped sweating, her skin was cool to touch, and her eyes had all but glossed over. Terre desperately wanted to get her to a medical center. She needed professional help, but there was no way that would happen now. The best he could hope for would be to manage the symptoms and give her some time to rest. Maybe there'd be something more they could do later.

Time was something she'd desperately need, but it was also a luxury they didn't have. All he could offer her was the time it would take to ensure Annika got to her sister okay, and so she continued to rest while he climbed higher.

Knowing what he knew now, it appeared to be a good thing he had continued on, rather than waiting with Becky. He'd first worried about leaving her alone in the stairwell in her condition. The swell of people below could break through the lock on the door if they were desperate enough, and he feared she would be trampled in the melee that followed. But even for a desperate crowd, it was a long climb.

Worse than that, if everyone on the casino floor were dead, the bots could come through themselves. Terre didn't know what purpose that would serve, though admittedly he didn't know what purpose killing the people in the casino held either. After the Sentinels shot down the masses, would they go scouting for survivors?

Terre shook his head, trying to wipe images of bodies flailing across the gaming tables out of his head—something easier said than done. Memories of the bodies would be embedded in his mind forever, just like the explosions at the base in Guam that took his wife and daughter from him. Just like the Onyx drones that had attacked San Francisco and left thousands dying in the street. Just like the plane that had fallen out of midair onto the freeway, bodies spilling out of its fuselage and not a parachute among them.

It had been something no man should ever have had to witness.

Terre had considered leaving his weapon with Becky, but he'd thought better of it. As he watched the obviously drunken man escort Annika out of the stairwell, he was extremely grateful he hadn't. He hated the thought of having to use a weapon, especially on a person, but after hearing the vile spewing from the pervert's mouth, Terre was ready to use whatever force was necessary to protect Annika. He just had to do so without her getting hurt in the process.

Once the door to the stairwell creaked shut, he crept up the stairs, blaster drawn. He was sure the man had been slurring his words, but it was hard to tell with the echo the stairwell produced. If he was drunk, there was no telling what irrational thoughts the man was having, aside from what seemed to be his normal depravity. Something else the stranger had said didn't sit right with him, either: comments referring to *we*. There was more going on than a crazed gunman, and he hadn't been sitting in the stairwell just waiting for a wayward woman to kidnap. Terre held his breath as he considered what else might be at play in the Grand Kawa resort.

In San Francisco, the National Guard and Homeland Security had done an excellent job of keeping gang members, looters, and opportunists looking to take advantage of the situation to a minimum. Here, it sounded as though the attack on the city was just getting started, and the Vegas Strip offered a lot of places for people to hide. Would the Guard be able to keep up? And would they be able to get a handle on things if more than one city was being attacked simultaneously? If Sentinels were on the move in both Vegas and New York, Terre suspected there would be other places under siege as well.

He inhaled deeply. The scent of paint lingered from the walls, as did the stench from spilled alcohol, food, and sex, which already emanated from the carpeting. His heart raced with adrenaline, anticipating the confrontation. Terre swore he could feel the nanobots in his blood vessels working overtime to keep him focused. Any tiredness from his earlier encounters had disappeared.

The door to the forty-second floor was a solid dark gray metal barrier, exactly like every other door on each of the forty-one floors before it.

Terre leaned against it, pressing his ear to the frame, straining to hear anything from the other side that might give him a clue as to what awaited him. Without the typical hum of electricity, there were no sounds coming from the other side whatsoever. After several moments had passed, he slowly pulled down the handle and opened the door.

Emergency lights from the hall revealed themselves, as did the crisp burgundy carpet.

There was no sign of Annika or the man who had hauled her away at gunpoint. He could feel his pulse slowing as he was able to release some tension in the death grip on his blaster.

If only the nanos would calm his nerves.

Now, the only problem was, he didn't know which direction they'd gone.

Terre glanced briefly at the map posted next to the stairwell for fire safety protocols. The floor's layout was identical to the one he was staying on several floors below. He'd been tempted to duck into his suite and grab a few things on his way up, but getting out was more of a priority than a handful of clothes and gear that wouldn't do him any good where he was going.

Despite his vague familiarity, Terre did his best to memorize the map as he pushed forward. The main hall was essentially a square, straightforward enough despite a few jagged turns to give the illusion there was a more prolific shape to it. Then, from each corner of the square jutted a long diagonal hall leading to four separate towers.

It looked simple on the map, but he knew the building was monstrous. He was going to have to get lucky to find Annika.

The hall was void of noise, other than his own still heavy breathing from the climb. He used the hem of his shirt sleeve to dry his sweaty face. With only emergency power on, the building was heating up in the blistering desert sun without the AC that normally kept the temperature in check. In that way, at least, it was good the sun was setting soon, but it meant they'd have to flee the city at night.

He took a deep breath. *One problem at a time.*

He had to pick a direction, and, with no real clue as to which way they might have gone, Terre decided any direction was better than none. He turned to his right and rounded the corner. The only consideration he had was that if the gunman had been planning something more nefarious, he'd likely want a view of the Strip. So, Terre decided he'd start with the east wing and work his way around.

He hadn't been too far behind them. Terre grabbed the robot pendant that hung around his neck.

Hopefully his lucky charm would come in handy after all.

Chapter Eighteen

Annika

Spring had barely broken the day Annika had received the text from her best friend, Neva. Neva's crush, Peter, was going to be off-roading down to the marsh next to their land to blow up a beaver dam messing with their irrigation system.

As a thirteen-year-old, anything new was an experience that had the potential to ingrain itself in your psyche and define the rest of your life. That day was no exception. It wasn't life-altering in the way a first kiss or winning a swim meet might have been, but it was certainly a day Annika would never forget.

Having grown up on a farm, dealing with the occasional nuisance caused by wild animals was nothing new. Usually, they would simply scare them away. Deer would get into the corn, or bears would walk through their yard on the way to forage for Saskatoon berries by the nearby stream. Prairie dogs burrowed holes in the field that would disrupt the navigation of their farm equipment or blow a tire. Once or twice that Annika could remember, a bobcat would attack their sheep, though she had never seen one of the majestic cats, only the bloody aftermath. Memories of her childhood were filled with her dad rushing out with a rifle, firing a warning shot, and the creature would be on its way. They would set air cannons up in particularly active seasons of birds and deer, though they weren't as effective at protecting the livestock.

Until that point, Annika had never heard of someone removing beaver dams from a property.

She would never forget the buckets of explosive aluminum powder and oxidizer. The smell of burning metal and plastic, mixed with wet wood and mildew from the dam itself. The pressure she had felt in her eyes and her chest as the force of the blow had reached where she sat, even a few hundred meters away.

Peter and his dad had howled with satisfaction in the aftermath. The explosion had sent pieces of wood and dirt sailing seventy to eighty feet in the air. This was obviously a highlight for these men as well, so she hadn't felt bashful about being astounded by the spectacle. Neva's eyes had widened with dismay at what she had just witnessed, but she'd forced an uncomfortable smile when Peter turned to her.

If the beavers had been the victims, Annika would have been horrified, too. But Peter had assured her they had waited until the animals were absent. They were just removing their handiwork to get the water flowing the way it needed to again. So, as a thirteen-year-old gazing upon that creek, her memories were of delight and amazement at the controlled catastrophe.

The complete opposite of what struck her now: pure horror.

Her jaw dropped, the memories flooding back to her as the stranger who had hauled her down the hall at gunpoint opened the door to the hotel room, revealing stacks of plastic explosives. Bricks, buckets, and wires lined the wall against the window, along with firearms leaning along the side of the room. The same metallic smell she remembered from the beaver dam wafted into the hall, and Annika's stomach roiled. She'd never forget how those homemade devices looked or smelled. And these looked much more sophisticated than the barnyard bombs Peter and his father had had at their disposal on the farm.

And there were *far* more of them.

"Harold! What the hell are you doing?" a man's rough voice called out from the room before she'd even realized there was anyone inside. In Annika's mind, the gruff accent sounded like it was from Boston, or at least somewhere in the northeastern United States. She always had a hard time pinpointing accents and had no experience other than from old movies.

The unfamiliar man stood from the work he had been doing on a laptop on a small table in the corner of the room. There was no concern evident on his face about his room being filled with explosives, only for Harold and the frightened young woman he now had in tow. This man had a bit more of a sophisticated edge to him than the drunk who still gripped her arm. A slim-fitting, deep red t-shirt was an advertisement for a chain of workout facilities. The muscular frame beneath the shirt highlighted he likely frequented the establishment.

"She was in the stairwell, Frank," Harold said. "I thought we could have a little fun while we wait for the signal. You know, one last hurrah?"

"Geez, Harold," he said, his fists curling. "Have you been drinking? You're supposed to be watching the exit for bots, not picking up women!"

"I've been waiting there all day. The power's out, and the bots are killing people. How long are we going to wait, anyway? Shouldn't we be stopping things before they get out of hand?"

Too late for that, Annika thought.

"We wait until we get the signal. Cuff her to the bed and get back to your post. That gun is to stop bots if they come first, not to intimidate strangers."

"These bots are armor-plated," Annika said, before she could stop herself. She didn't look up, but she could feel their eyes turn on her.

"And what do you know of it?" Frank barked. "You wanna protect them?"

Her eyes darted to the explosives and back to the man, who seemed angrier, though perhaps less of a pervert, than Harold. The pieces refused to come together in her mind. These men seemed opposed to the bots, just like Terre and Hailey. Why were they holed up in the hotel with enough explosives to take out half the building?

They're going to bring it down.

The thought slapped her as if out of nowhere, but the justification eluded her. Regardless of their reasoning, these men were planning to blow up the hotel.

And she was going to be in the room when they did it. Cheyenne, six floors above them, was going to die in the blast, too.

"I was in the street when they started firing on the crowd. Bullets didn't even slow them down."

Annika risked a glance up at the two men, who stood looking at each other with confused snarls on their faces.

"Figures," Frank said. "Harold, lock her up."

Harold cringed, though he eyed the minibar with a lustful eye, which seemed to bring his spirits up. He dragged her to the bedframe and unlinked one cuff before pulling it around the foot of the bed and re-cuffing her hand.

He took two steps toward the kitchen before Frank yelled at him again.

"No more booze, numb nuts! You can barely stand as it is. Make sure nobody else comes in here. I don't want any surprises. Radio me if you see so much as a room service bot. Understand?"

Harold mumbled several obscenities under his breath, most of which Annika was thankful she couldn't hear, and stumbled out of the room.

Annika was on the floor next to the bed, her hands above her head, resting on the post they were chained to. She shifted several times, but there was only one position she could adopt that wasn't excruciatingly uncomfortable. It wouldn't take long for her wrists to go numb as the blood vacated her hands, but if there was anything she could be thankful for, it was that she could give her legs a rest.

"I regret ever bringing that clown along," Frank muttered once Harold had left the room. Annika wasn't sure if he was talking to himself or her. He'd probably been cooped up in the room for so long that he was happy to talk to anyone with an ounce of sobriety.

Perhaps she could use it to her advantage.

"Did you cause the power outage?" Annika asked, thinking she might as well try to learn something. "The Strip is in chaos. Are you behind all of this?"

Frank snorted in derision. "No," he said, pushing back one of the slatted blinds so he could peer out the window. Annika got enough of a glimpse to know the room faced the Strip. "That was an unlucky coincidence. Though, if we play our cards right, it might work in our favor."

"Then why do you want to blow up the hotel?" she asked. "It sounds like you're planning on going down with it."

"Not if I can help it." Frank moved to the window, as though only half invested in the conversation. "Though I don't think Tweedle-dee is going to be capable of stumbling down the stairs fast enough, the state he's in."

"But why?" she repeated.

Frank turned from the window and looked at her, his shoulders slumped as if he had forgotten for a moment who he had been talking to.

"Cause they're trying to get rid of us. They've built and run this hotel on bots alone. What are the rest of us supposed to do? They've taken trucking jobs, retail, receptionists ... Hell, you can't even order a pizza without a bot delivering it to you. You might be too young to remember the days when some zit-faced kid would show up to your door; now, you get this little bot wheeling around the city instead. *Bah!*" Frank waved his hand as if it wasn't worth the effort of trying to explain it to her.

"What are you talking about? Who are 'they'?"

"Take your pick," he said. Frank grabbed a backpack and loaded several handguns and clothes inside. "The government, corporations, globalists ... They're all working together to cut us out. Once the bots have replaced us all, you think they're going to keep giving us money to do nothing? Where's this money coming from if nobody's working?"

Annika shook her head, unsure of how to respond.

"We'll be obsolete. They'll have full control, and they won't even need us to do their dirty work.

"So, what are we gonna do?" He continued without pause, as though he couldn't help himself. "Wave our little signs in the air and hope it all goes back to the way it was? Huh? Once they've automated us away, there will be no going back. We need to take a stand. We need to let them know they can't make humans obsolete."

Annika didn't interrupt. She had heard enough anti-bot sentiment her entire life to understand the man's outrage. Bots were taking their jobs, taking over the farms, and soon there would be nothing left for humans to do. Her entire presentation at the conference had been intended to quell some of that anger; to keep employees calm as they watched their friends, family, and colleagues become unemployed.

Maybe she had been complicit. But what could she do about it? Blowing up a hotel certainly wasn't the answer.

"And now, with this fighting," Frank waved at the street below, and through the crack in the curtains, Annika could see the haze of smoke masking properties across the Strip. Pops of gunfire and the buzz of the bots' ray guns could be heard faintly from the street. "It's just the next step. You think these weaponized bots in the street are here by accident? It's all planned. If they kill enough of us off, there's less of us to support for doin' nothin'. A win-win for them. Hopefully, we can take enough of them with us to make them think twice."

The sweat on Annika's back had grown cold, making her shirt damp, and adding to her discomfort. Her hands were numb to the point where she could no longer feel the cuffs digging into them—just the pins and needles from the loss of circulation. The man was talking about causing a terrorist attack to protest *job losses*, of all things.

"What about the thousands of people the blast will kill? Don't they matter?"

"Look, sister, there's collateral damage in every war. The people staying here are supportin' the greedy bastards." Frank pointed to the floor to emphasize his point. "We make a statement here and now, and no one's gonna want to stay in a robot hotel for a very, very long time. Who knows, maybe we can turn humanity off robot workers all together. Damned if they don't stop military development."

Shouts from the street below were barely audible. Frank pulled the curtain back further to take another look.

"What's happening down there?" she asked.

"Lots of dead people," he said.

Frank backed away from the window and turned to the wall, pulled back his fist, and threw a punch. A sharp crack followed, leaving a dent in the drywall. Frank shook his hand. "You're so worried what we're doin' here's gonna kill people? They're already dead. There's a few cops doing their best, but I don't see the military or anyone else helping."

Annika took his moment of distraction to test her handcuffs. The pole of the bedframe seemed solid enough. It would take more than a good kick to break free.

Her eyes went back to the stacks of explosives and weapons. Frank was clearly unhinged, and thousands more were going to die if he had his way. But she didn't want to be here when it was time to light the fuse.

"Who are you working for?" she asked on a whim.

Frank turned his head and looked at her with a scoff. "What are you, a cop?" he asked. "Enough with the questions."

"I'm not a cop," she said, her eyes downcast. She should've been smarter with her line of questioning—perhaps she could have learned more. "What do you plan to do with me?"

"Nothing," he said, straight-faced. "I don't plan to do nothing with you. Harold's an idiot. He shouldn't have brought you here."

"So, you'll let me go?" she said, pushing down the hope that rose within her.

"What? No. You've seen too much; we can't let you go. When we get the signal, we'll leave—but you'll stay here."

Her heart stopped and her mind raced as Annika searched for the right thing to say. *Anything* that might get her out of the hotel room.

"I won't tell anyone, I swear." She wanted to cry out about her sister, maybe gain his sympathies if she told him there was a young girl's life at stake. But the depraved look she'd seen in Harold's eye earlier convinced her these terrorists were perverts first and foremost, and she didn't want to pull Cheyenne down with her.

"You're damn right you won't. You won't be leaving this room, sister. You'll be stuck here, just like everyone else in this damned bot hotel."

Annika had surmised as much, but her heart still sank. Somehow, she needed to get out. The handcuffs dug at her wrists as she tugged at them. She tried to slip her hands through the openings to no avail, pinching and bruising her skin in the process.

A radio crackled on the bedside table. Annika hadn't noticed the black box sitting there until it sprang to life. It appeared that Frank and Harold weren't working alone after all.

"Frankie, you there?" a woman's voice crackled over the speaker.

"Geez, woman," Frank muttered as he walked over and snatched up the radio. His back was turned to Annika for the first time, muscles rippling beneath his t-shirt. Far from the sloppy drunk Harold was, Frank was well put together and had some athleticism to him.

"I told you, no names," he yelled into the device. "What do ya want?"

A few moments of silence dragged on before the radio crackled to life again. Annika held her breath; she expected she knew what was coming.

"It's a madhouse here," the woman's voice said. "The floor's crawling with people. The demons are shooting their way through every hotel on the Strip. We need to do this now."

"What about the others? Are all the packages secure?" Frank asked.

"So far," the woman said. "Every one's accounted for.

We're going to set the timers for forty minutes. Honestly, it's more time than I'd like, but you know how navigating the Strip can be, especially with the mayhem the bots have caused. I'd prefer to get you guys out of there."

"What if Security finds it before it goes?" Frank asked. "They could shut the whole thing down."

"Security's got their hands full—they won't be able to find and stop them all. Just set the timer and get out of there!"

A round of machine gun fire, followed by distant shouting, crackled on the other end of the radio.

"There's a lotta ruckus going on down there," Frank said. "Is the rendezvous still the same?"

"Right now, assume nothing's changed. I'll contact you if it does. End transmission."

Frank set the radio down and got to work. He punched several keys on the laptop, which still sat on the table. Though the screen was pointed at her, Annika couldn't see what he was doing from her vantage point.

The man carefully picked up a wire that led to the explosives, plugged it into the computer, and logged some more keystrokes.

"Sorry, lady," Frank said as he picked up several of the rifles that leaned against the wall. "This is where we say goodbye. You've got thirty minutes. I suggest you make your peace with whatever higher power you believe in."

Her eyes focused on the laptop, its screen now clearly visible. Large black digits flashed over the monitor—*39:39* —and were rapidly counting down.

Frank grabbed the backpack he had packed moments before and then slung three rifles over his shoulders. Annika assumed one was for Harold, but with these people, who knew?

"And if you somehow manage to get free, don't even think

about unplugging that wire. There's a failsafe that'll cause the whole thing to blow. Just run."

"Why not let me go?" she said. "No one will ever have to know!"

"Sorry, sis. You've seen my face. I ain't gonna take that risk. I should shoot you now so you can't escape. But that ain't my style."

Without giving her the opportunity to argue, Frank shoved a gag in her mouth and tied it behind her head. He moved to open the door to the hall and then slipped out.

Annika watched the digital countdown and wondered what the hell she was going to do.

Chapter Nineteen

Terre

TERRE HAD JUST TURNED the corner of the hallway in time to see the man who had taken Annika away at gunpoint wobble down the hall, presumably heading back to the stairwell where Terre had last seen him.

Annika wasn't with him.

It hadn't taken long for Terre to scour the eastern towers with no luck. He must have passed the room they were keeping her in. If only he had seen which door the gunman had come out of!

Terre gripped the robot pendant that hung around his neck. Sarah had always told him it was his lucky charm, but since the attack in Guam, he hadn't felt very lucky.

But if he had an ounce of luck left in him, this would be a good time to use it.

The gunman's footsteps disappeared, and Terre took it as an all-clear to creep back down the hall.

There were two towers separate from the main loop of the central building, and he figured he might as well start with the south tower. So, he crept in that direction, keeping his ears pricked for any sign of where the woman was being held. He didn't know what he expected to hear. There were likely some guests who had holed up in their rooms until the power was restored. Terre didn't expect too many of them would decide to walk down forty-two flights of stairs if they thought they'd have to journey back up them.

Annika could literally be in any room, and short of busting open doors, one at a time, he was running out of options.

For all Terre knew, she could be unconscious—or dead. He shuddered at the thought of stumbling across her body— if he found anything at all. It did little to console him that he hadn't heard any gunshots on his last circuit of the floor. No matter how big the complex was, he'd still have heard those, especially if he had been on the same side of the building.

But there were quieter ways to kill someone.

His mind scrambled as he considered everything that might have gone horribly wrong. What would he do if Annika was dead? Her sister still needed help, but would she leave with a total stranger?

One footstep after another, he crept along the quiet hallway. Disheartened, he dragged his feet. It was almost too quiet. Without the hum of electricity flowing through the walls, he could hear what felt like every crack of the building. He strained for signs of something—*anything*—to indicate Annika might be alive.

Nothing presented itself.

When he turned the corner to the north tower, an athletic man with muscles Terre could only dream of having had just stepped out of a room. He was the first person Terre had seen, other than the gunman who'd taken Annika. Three rifles hung from his shoulders, as well as a pack slung over a deep red t-shirt.

Not suspicious at all.

This newcomer looked much more capable than the

bumbling fool that had accosted Annika, so Terre briefly questioned whether the two could really be connected. But it was the only lead he had to go on.

Terre ducked into a doorway, hoping the newcomer would head toward the stairwell and take no notice of him. The less attention he could draw to himself, the better. And there was no point alerting the fully-loaded man to his presence.

The thudding of the man's footsteps faded as he rounded the corner and sped down the hall. Guns bounced precariously beside him, and he only seemed vaguely concerned about their movement.

Terre retraced the man's steps, ducking into the north tower hall, avoiding the possibility that the stranger might turn around and spot him. Luck, it seemed, was on his side, so far. He crept to the door the man had come out of.

He rapped on it three times and listened. A shuffle and a muffled yelp replied. The voice was unintelligible. The originator could have been saying "come in" or "get lost" or anything in between. It could have been the television.

He'd have to take a chance.

Terre pulled at the door handle. No luck.

He grabbed the CD-115 blaster from his hip and aimed it at the lock. Shooting at another person might be something he was hesitant to do, but he had no qualms about melting a lock.

It took only seconds for the beam to melt the lock and the door to pop open.

Terre struggled to comprehend the scene laid out before him. The emergency lighting from the hall streamed through the doorway. Annika was sitting on the floor next to the bed, her wrists held in the air above her head and handcuffed to its footboard. Wide-eyed in horror, she looked at him without a shred of recognition of the face peering in from the hallway. Though the emergency lights were dim, they were practically blinding compared to the darkness of the hotel room. The shades had been drawn, and the only other source of light came from a laptop sitting open on a table placed awkwardly in the center of the room.

Annika had been gagged, and it appeared she was bleeding from her wrists, though Terre couldn't make out whether the blood stemmed from her handcuffs digging in or another injury. Dirt and sweat had been smeared across her face, and her short blonde hair was matted and grimy.

Terre completed a quick scan of the room to ensure there was nobody else waiting to ambush him. His pulse quickened as his grasp tightened on the grip of the CD-115. As he stepped into the shadows and shut the door, relief flooded Annika's face as the light behind him revealed his face.

Satisfied there was nobody else in the room, Terre tucked the weapon back into his belt and rushed to Annika's side. He squatted next to her and untied the crude gag that had been wedged into her mouth.

Annika sucked in the air around her, as though she had been struggling to breathe through her nose.

"Are you okay?" Terre asked her. "Did they hurt you?"

"I'm a little shaken, but I'm all right. For now," Annika wheezed, shaking off the effects of the gag. "We need to get out of here!"

"Easy now. Let's get those handcuffs off first. And you're going to want to take it slow."

"There's no time!" Annika's eyes looked up at him pleadingly as they reflected squares of light from the laptop's screen. "Once that timer reaches zero, this hotel's going to blow!"

Terre's eye was drawn to the computer on the table. The large numbers on its display were counting down to something that was barely over thirty minutes away. He swore as he noticed the wire running from the laptop to the stack of bricks and buckets piled in the corner of the room. He had never seen homemade explosives before, but it wasn't hard to deduce what the items were.

Terre pushed himself off his knees and stepped cautiously toward the table. "Can't we just disconnect it?"

"*Don't!*" Annika exclaimed, trying to jump to her feet. Her hands were still tied to the bedframe, causing her to double over. "Unplugging it will set it off!"

"Okay! Okay!" Terre said, his hands out, motioning to her that he wasn't going to touch the thing. "Maybe there's a way to stop the clock."

"This isn't the only one," Annika said. "There are others. It'd be a waste of time. We need to get to Cheyenne and get the hell out of here."

The counter continued to tick down. They had about thirty minutes—and a lot of stairs between them and safety. Annika's eyes pleading with him to leave the ticking timebomb alone.

"What the hell have you gotten yourself into?" Terre asked.

A small desk was situated against the wall. He needed something to pick the lock of the handcuffs; a paperclip would suffice.

"What are you looking for?" Annika asked.

"I need a wire or pin to get you out of those cuffs."

"Will a bobby pin work?" she asked. "I've got a few in my hair. Go ahead and pull one out."

"That's perfect," Terre said. He closed the distance between them and pulled a pin from her hair. The woman smelled of sweat, dirt, and a hint of alcohol, perhaps bourbon. It was faint, though, so he shrugged it off as something else, possibly tired perfume.

Ideally, he'd want to work with a pair of pliers, but his

options were limited. Terre worked the ends of the bobby pin off with his teeth and then shaped the pin to a forty-five degree angle.

"Do you actually know what you're doing?" Annika asked. "Or are you just messing around?"

"We're about to find out, aren't we?" Terre liked to keep the mystery around his skill from others, but the reason he could pick locks was much more benign than most would imagine. His father had been a locksmith and had taught him how to open a basic lock when he was a boy. From there, his interest grew, and he began working with locks as a hobby. He grew up believing he'd be a locksmith, just like his dad, until his father had slowly lost more and more work to robots. They did the job at half the cost, so the work for humans dried up. There was no future in the business, and Terre soon realized the only secure path forward was in computing.

And he even wondered about that sometimes.

But as picking locks was his one party trick, Terre kept it to himself until he needed it. Then again, there weren't too many situations in day-to-day life where he found it a valuable skill to have. Not until lately, at least.

The lock on the cuffs clicked open.

Annika wasted no time in jumping up and heading for the door.

"Hang on a sec," Terre said, grabbing his backpack and rummaging through it.

"What are you doing? Don't you see the clock? We don't have time…"

Terre tossed her a water bottle. "You're still dehydrated."

Annika grabbed the bottle in midair and didn't hesitate to open it and start chugging. "Thank you," she said in between gulps.

"What's going on here?" he asked, taking advantage of a

few moments of respite before they pressed ahead. "Who's doing this?"

"I don't know who they are," Annika said, tossing her empty bottle onto the bed. "All they told me was that they've planned a terrorist attack to scare people away from staying in a hotel run by bots."

Terre scoffed. "I don't think they'll have to worry about that anytime soon. The bots have pretty much taken care of that by themselves."

He rubbed his forehead; the day continued to go from bad to worse. He stepped over to the blinds and peered out onto the Strip, fearful of what might wait below. Carnage, as he had expected. Dust still hung in the air from downed pedestrian passes and building decor, which now lay strewn along the sidewalks, along with the bodies. Dozens of bodies haphazardly lay across the sidewalk and into the street. Maintenance bots were busy cleaning them up without a care as to the nature of their refuse, programmed to remove anything that blocked the sidewalk.

Given what he had seen earlier, Terre was surprised there weren't more deceased.

The Sentinels—for now, at least—were nowhere to be seen. Terre suspected they would be going through each casino, extending their purge. Police bots were rolling along the sidewalks with their guns extended, though Terre couldn't tell if they were looking for Sentinels or humans at this point. Perhaps they'd have enough of a window to cross the Strip on their way out of the city.

"There are other devices," Annika repeated. "They've got more at other hotels. We've got … twenty-seven minutes. That's not a lot of time to be enjoying the view."

"If we're going to get out of this place," Terre answered, "I want to know what we're heading into."

"And?" she asked. "How bad is it?"

"The Sentinels appear to have moved inside. If we can steer clear of them, it might buy us enough time to get out of the city."

He turned back to the room, ready to move on, but something in the skyline caught his eye.

His luck, it seemed, had run out.

"*Onyx*," he said, barely louder than a whisper. "These explosives might be the least of our worries."

Two black orbs were heading toward the city. Fast.

Whatever he and K had accomplished during the upload at Berkeley, it hadn't appeared to have stopped the death machines. It was hard to judge how far away the Onyx were against the backdrop of the mammoth hotels and desert mountains in the distance, but if Terre had to guess, they had about a half hour until they arrived.

Chapter Twenty

Terre

THE ROAR of jet engines over the city indicated a counterstrike was already being prepared.

"When these bombs go off," Terre said, "the party might just be getting started."

"What do you mean?" Annika asked. "What's going on?"

"Reinforcements are coming," he replied.

"I don't understand. Coming for who?"

"Didn't you see the footage from San Francisco? The bots that attacked the city?"

Color fled from Annika's face as she nodded. "The flying black spheres with ray guns?"

"Those are the ones," Terre said, closing the blinds.

"What do we do?"

"One problem at a time," he said. "For now, let's get you and your sister out of here. Then we'll worry about getting out of the path of the death machines."

The flurry of threats dazed Annika enough that she chose not to ask questions, for which Terre was grateful. They needed to get moving before this device detonated— or before the Onyx had a chance to get there first.

Death by either man or bot is still death all the same.

"Go get Cheyenne," he said. "We'll meet you on the way down."

"You're not coming with me?"

"Becky's still on the landing a couple dozen floors down, in rough shape. I'll get her and start helping her down the stairs. If you want your friend to make it, she's going to need help. If I have to carry her down, I will. I'll meet you in the stairwell on the way down."

Hopefully, his nanos would help Terre lift more than he could unassisted. Becky wasn't a large woman, but carrying anyone down twenty flights of stairs would be a herculean feat.

Annika had opened the door to the hall partway, but then paused and turned to Terre as if processing what he was saying.

"I need you to come with me," she said.

"Why? Are you hurt? It'll be faster if we split up."

Annika shook her head. "No, I need you and your ray gun. I don't know if Cheyenne is safe, or if I'll be safe going up there."

"What do you mean?"

"Cheyenne has a bot with her."

TERRE LISTENED INTENTLY as they raced down the hall, Annika breathlessly recounting bits and pieces of the story of how her parents had died in a fire in the middle-of-nowhere Canada and how they had received a support bot through a Canadian government trial project. Terre had only heard of these Keepers once before, while Fredricks had been briefing him and K about the Sentinels. The Sentinels were based on the Keepers' schematics and software.

"I'm worried that whatever's causing those bots on the street to malfunction is going to happen to Ember."

A bot with a name, Terre thought, though he supposed it wasn't uncommon. Families had been naming those damn robot dogs for years.

"You probably think I'm being ridiculous," she said. Annika's voice had cracked a few times during the story, her eyes wandering the halls as though unable to focus on anything around her. Terre had seen people go through this before, soldiers on base exhibiting early signs of PTSD. The stress of the day would be enough to kill anyone's spirit, but it seemed Annika had had past encounters with AI gone awry. And her sister being stuck in a room alone with a bot was naturally only antagonizing the situation.

"No," Terre said cautiously. He wanted to be optimistic, but he also wanted Annika to understand the gravity of their situation. "You've got reason to worry. Those bots on the streets were developed from the same spec as your Keeper."

Annika turned to look at him. She was one of the whitest girls he had ever seen, but he swore her face went three shades lighter.

"How is that possible? They look so ... so *different*. Those bots that attacked us ... that attacked your friend, Hailey. They look like warriors."

"I know," Terre replied, trying to offer a steady tone. "The military reworked their appearance, but their system schematics are the same."

"What is this? Some crazed Internet theory? How do you know so much about them?"

Terre sighed. "It's a long story. You remember me telling you I need to find someone? He's an old colleague of mine. He designed the program for your bot. He was Chief Engineer of NASA robotics, and he created the Keepers to be used for the space program. His work is up on Mars, helping the colonists to terraform the planet."

"He built the things shooting at us?"

Terre shook his head. "The military co-opted his designs; decided they'd be able to make better soldiers than world-builders. Now, we're left with the mess. Humans have a way of taking what's been designed to make the world better and using it to kill each other."

"What do you mean?" she asked.

"From the small bit Kristopher told me, the Keepers were babysitter bots, built to provide parents in the Mars colonization program with additional support. Unlike the Sentinels, they're not programmed for war and destruction. The chaos in the streets is because those bots were redesigned for warfare. I doubt your Keeper will turn out to be some sort of killer."

But, then again, what did he know? The military had been constructing a secret army of super sophisticated robots under everyone's nose, so anything was possible.

They reached the door to the stairwell. Terre pushed against the solid metal and reluctantly peered inside.

"I imagine those lunatics have fled the building," Terre said. "But I wonder if I should have left Becky alone? You probably have a better read on them than I do. Do you think they would have hurt Becky on the way down?"

Annika shrugged. "Frank didn't seem to want to be bothered with anyone. He was here to push the button on the timer and nothing else. Harold, on the other hand ..." She paused and shook her head. She felt disgusting even speaking their names, but Annika powered through. "I don't think Frank would have let them stop for any reason. He was pissed Harold had brought me to the room. If Becks didn't bother them, I think they will have left her alone. She'd just be another piece of collateral damage to them."

"Let's pray that's the case," Terre said. "I promised to get you *both* out of here, and I intend to keep that promise."

They had half a dozen flights of stairs to go. Terre couldn't help but continually check his watch. They were going to be cutting it close.

Very close.

After everything she had been through, Annika had to be running on pure adrenaline. It surprised Terre she could even stand, never mind bound up the stairs in a determined fashion. But every step was another inch closer to getting her sister and getting them out of this death trap.

The only problem was, they'd then be stepping into a war zone.

Terre struggled to ignore the chaos that was still erupting outside the hotel. They had to focus on one problem at a time, but their time to make a critical decision about how to leave was drawing nearer.

Annika cleared two or three steps at a time. Terre would normally have worried about her overexerting herself, but they didn't have the time for caution. Every step mattered.

They burst onto the forty-eighth floor. There was nothing to distinguish it from the floors below: the same red carpeting, the same red and gold wallpaper. Even the paintings on the walls were identical.

Once again, they pushed to the west side of the tower, Annika now in a full-blown sprint. She stumbled a few times over the patterned carpet, her legs pushing her further than their normal level of endurance.

As they reached the door that presumably accessed Annika's suite, she fumbled to find her keycard in her pants pocket, her hands shaking as she tapped it on the pad on the door.

"Cheyenne? Grab your things! We've got to get out of

here," Annika called into the room as she burst in and stopped short.

The room was empty.

Chapter Twenty-One

Annika

ANNIKA GASPED for breath as the shock hit her in the gut like a baseball bat.

"Cheyenne!" She frantically scoured the room, moving from the closet to the bathroom and even under the bed.

"Where is she? I don't understand. Where could they have gone?"

The room was neat and tidy, as though it hadn't been occupied that day. That wasn't like Cheyenne at all.

"They haven't been here for a while," Terre offered. "Is it possible the bot could have taken her somewhere earlier in the day?"

Annika shook her head, running her palms through her short blonde hair. The dirt and grime pulled off her scalp with the pressure, some of it falling onto the laminate flooring below. Her heart raced along with her mind.

The bed had been made, and the blinds had been drawn. Their luggage had been piled neatly off to the side of the room, as if it had never been opened. On the counter sat Cheyenne's eye-piece.

"No, this is all wrong. I talked to her right before the

power went out." Annika's lungs felt heavy, unable to pull in enough air as she spoke. "We were texting, making plans for supper. Ember wouldn't have taken her out of the room without at least telling me. And Cheyenne? She's not exactly messy, but she still wouldn't have left things so tidy. Someone's trying to make it look like they hadn't been here. But why?"

Annika rubbed her face as she sat on the bed, desperately racking her brain for answers. Terre continued to study the suite, as if hoping for a clue she had overlooked.

The room wasn't massive, but it was extensive enough that Annika hadn't felt too guilty about leaving Cheyenne there. A black couch sat against the wall, with a desk next to it. A widescreen TV sat across from the bed. It was more a small bachelor apartment than it was a hotel room, with a small counter separating the main room from a kitchenette. Even in the deluxe suites, they didn't provide you with a means to cook for yourself. They wanted you to eat at the resorts.

Terre glanced at his watch as he strolled into the bathroom. Annika knew he was worrying about the time left on the explosives, but her mind was frozen. She couldn't comprehend that her sister had vanished without a trace.

She had failed Cheyenne. Just like she had failed her parents.

She had failed everyone.

"Why is the bathtub filled with water?" he asked.

"Cheyenne would have filled it when the power went out. It's the first thing we do back home. You want to save a large supply of clean water, just in case it doesn't come back on for a few days."

Growing up in the prairies proved to have had no shortage of emergencies. For the last few decades, it was a nonstop assault of fires, floods, tornadoes, locusts, and whatever other biblical plague could be dreamed up. It was a wonder anyone still chose to live there.

Terre glanced across the room one more time. "So, she would have still been here when the power went out?"

"Yeah? So?"

"The bot is programmed to keep Cheyenne safe, right? That's why you have it? As a protector?"

Annika couldn't bring herself to do anything other than nod. Tears had filled her eyes, but they had yet to leak down onto her cheeks. She didn't have the energy to cry. Cheyenne had been her charge, and now her sister had disappeared with a bot she had accepted into their home. She had let her parents down again.

"If the bot somehow detected a threat," Terre continued, "either from the explosives, the Onyx, or whatever else might be coming that we haven't discovered yet, perhaps it tried to take the kid to safety."

Annika barely registered his comment. Her mind flowed in the hues of oranges and reds filling the room as the sun made its way down the horizon. Her sister was gone; that was all she could focus on. There had to be something else she could do.

"Either way," Terre said, staring at his watch, "we've got less than fifteen minutes to get out of here before the entire place blows. We need to leave."

Annika didn't move; she couldn't even nod.

She was suddenly a teenager again, watching the flames bearing down on the farm. Her parents were within its destructive glow. She was helpless to save them, only able to watch the flames as the RCMP rescued her and Cheyenne from their soon-to-be ablaze home and forced them onto the bus that would take her away from them forever.

The orange and red glow danced around her, tormenting her with gleeful scorn. She should have stopped her parents;

she should have forced them to evacuate when the sirens came. But she hadn't, and now they were dead.

Just like Cheyenne. Once again, she had failed.

Terre grabbed Annika's shoulders and forced himself into her line of vision, breaking her glossy gaze. She glanced around, quickly orienting herself, and came back to her senses.

"There's no sign of a struggle; no reason to think your bot would have hurt her. Isn't it far more likely it would have taken Cheyenne to safety?"

Annika knew what Terre was saying made sense, but her thoughts were cloudy, like they belonged to someone else. Her mind raced from one scenario to the next, unable to focus.

"Here," Terre said. He reached into his pack and pulled out a protein bar.

Without considering what she was doing, Annika tore off the blue wrapper and took a bite. The surge of sugar and flavor brought her new life, and she looked down at the bar in her hand. She hadn't eaten for hours.

"Thanks," she said. "I don't think I realized how hungry I was."

"We've got to move," Terre said, barely batting an eye. "Let's get going."

Annika's mind raced as she surveyed the room one more time. There had to be a clue, a hint … *something*.

"But Cheyenne! What if she's still in the building?" Annika looked at Terre pleadingly. There had to be a way to ensure her sister was all right. She wouldn't be able to live with herself if the building came down on top of her.

"And what if she's not? Would she want you to die looking for her? Even if the bot *didn't* take her someplace safe, we'll never find her before the place blows. If she's safe, Cheyenne will be left alone."

Annika's shoulders slumped. He made a good point. If Ember had sensed a threat and had escorted Cheyenne out of the hotel, she would need her sister. Annika was the only family Cheyenne had.

She should never have brought Cheyenne to Vegas. She had ignored the warning in her gut. The media had promised the situation with the rogue bots had been dealt with and the threat toward herself and her sister had seemed so insignificant, yet here they were, forced to live out her darkest nightmare.

Terre was right; she wouldn't help Cheyenne by getting herself killed. And, chances were, whether well-intentioned or not, Ember had likely taken her sister outside. Annika wished she knew what the bot was up to, and why she had packed up the room so neatly before they'd left. If there was such an enormous threat, wouldn't they have left as quickly as possible? She ran a hand through her short hair and sighed. "If my parents were alive, they would be so mad at me for bringing her here. I should have let her stay with a friend."

"Your parents would be proud of you for bringing her this far."

Annika raised an eyebrow. "You hardly know me." She was still unsure of what to think of the man who had injected himself into her search. Knowing nothing about her, Terre had shown up and saved her life twice. Despite there being hundreds of other people dying all around them, he'd chosen to help her rather than anyone else, including the woman who had showed up with him. The more Annika thought about it, Terre seemed to have a callous side to him. Hailey had seemingly sacrificed herself so the three of them could get into the hotel, and he had barely batted an eye at her heroism.

"That's true," he replied. "But I can already tell there isn't anything you wouldn't do to protect Cheyenne." Terre let out a sigh, holding onto the mysterious pendant he kept around his neck. "I know what that's like. I let down the one I was supposed to protect, too."

It was a side of him Annika hadn't seen. Instead of the brash, confident man of action, a moment of softness and regret had overtaken him, as though Terre were melting into a memory he refused to leave behind.

Annika nodded, deciding not to press him to share more about whatever incident he was referring to; there'd be time for that later. Her eyes dropped to the carpet, scanning it, hoping it would provide her with some answers. There were none to be found, though. The only thing that remained true was that she needed to find her sister. But Terre was right; it wouldn't help Cheyenne if she died.

"You're right," she said, confidence and strength returning to her voice. "So, I better not die in this place." She scarfed the last of her protein bar and took a swig of water to wash it down as they moved toward the door.

"How much time do we have?" she asked.

"Fifteen minutes," Terre replied, shaking his head in disbelief.

As they got to the doorway, Annika quickly swapped shoes. Her bright orange hiking shoes were nearly new and would provide much more comfort than the dress shoes she had on. Terre had mentioned fleeing the city, and she imagined having comfortable footwear would be a godsend.

She guiltily looked at Terre and his dusty cap-toe Oxfords. They looked built more for style than for comfort, but she didn't have an alternative to offer him.

They burst down the hall and back to the stairwell. Every

moment counted, and the ticking of Terre's watch echoed off the walls and rattled in her brain.

They flew down the stairs. There was no time to let the tiredness in her legs slow her; she had to keep moving. She lost count of how many floors they had covered before nearly tripping over Becky, who was leaning against the wall where they had left her.

A few empty water bottles sat next to her, along with a couple of blue wrappers from the same type of protein bar Terre had given Annika minutes before.

"I was beginning to worry you had forgotten about me!" Becky said, a smile on her face. "Why are you in such a hurry? Where's Cheyenne?"

Annika had to give her head a shake as she realized her friend had no idea what was happening. At least the woman appeared to be faring better.

"Long story, but we've got to get out—*now!* We'll explain on the way."

Annika grabbed Becky's arm and basically pulled her to the next set of stairs.

"I'm still feeling a bit dizzy," Becky said. "Can I sit this one out?"

"You're going to be feeling a bit *dead* if you don't come with us!" Terre barked as he worked his way past the two women. Despite continuing to save their butts, it was clear he would not get himself killed to do so. There wasn't any more time to sit around and discuss intentions.

"Come on," Annika said. "I'll make sure you don't fall."

Terre was already working his way down, making no qualms about not waiting for them. Every part of Annika was screaming danger, panic, and to get the hell out of the building, but she forced herself to pause and reach out a hand to the woman for support.

Becky seemed to take the cue that something more dire

was happening and allowed Annika to pull her down the stairs.

"Are you going to tell me what's going on?" Becky asked as they reached the next platform.

"Explosives are going to bring this whole place down on top of us," Annika replied, not masking the grit in her voice. "And if that doesn't work, the bots are on their way to finish the job."

Becky's face said it all, and her pace quickened significantly.

"What about Cheyenne?" Becky asked. Her words came in short bursts as she struggled to breathe under their hurried pace.

"She wasn't there," Annika replied. "We think Ember took her somewhere safer."

Or at least, that's what she hoped had happened.

Chapter Twenty-Two

Terre

TERRE BASICALLY FLUNG himself down the stairs, trusting the two women were still on his tail. He intentionally set a breakneck pace, knowing they'd match his urgency.

The prospect of what might await them when they reached the ground floor sent Terre's already elevated heart rate soaring. Would there be guests clogging the casino floor, preventing their escape? Or would the Sentinels have taken everyone else out and be waiting with blasters pointed at the stairwell?

There was only one way to find out.

And no matter the scenario, Terre wasn't looking forward to what it might entail.

With no time to panic, and no time to overthink their next steps, they had to get to the ground floor and to the nearest exit.

It felt like both an eternity and a split second before he had to face the demons that waited for them behind the door; the door that he had locked only minutes before. Annika and Becky stopped behind him as he reached it, their eyes wide in terror and their skin red with exertion. He hoped they somehow still had more reserve strength to pull them through what was to come.

"I don't know what's going to be waiting for us on the other side of this door," he said, the seconds still ticking by inside his head. "Get ready to duck, but more importantly, get ready to run like hell."

The two women nodded, and he broke the seal of the door frame, giving himself a moment to assess whatever situation awaited them.

The casino floor was quiet. There was the obvious silence from the void of electricity, slot machines, and music, but there was also no chatter, no screams, no gunfire, no blasters.

Nothing.

He pushed the door open a bit more.

"Back stairwell!" a man's voice yelled from somewhere on the floor. "Who's there? Identify yourself!"

Terre's pulse drummed in his head as he put up his hands and crept carefully out.

At least it's not a bot, he thought, though it did little to calm his nerves.

A man in green fatigues stood in the middle of the casino floor, a blaster weapon Terre didn't recognize aimed at his head. Terre took a quick scan of the building as best he could without straying too far from the man who was holding a gun to him. Dead bodies lay everywhere, both man and machine. It appeared they had cleared out most civilians, though—or at least any surviving ones.

Upon seeing a human face, the soldier lowered his weapon.

"It's all right!" he yelled behind him. Terre noticed there were other infantrymen spread throughout the casino, taking stock of the bots that lay incapacitated on the floor.

"Sir," Terre said, his voice urgent. The soldier didn't point the gun at him anymore, but with the prospect of its return, he was hesitant to make any sudden moves. "There's a bomb in the building. We have," he looked to his watch out of the side of his eye, cautious of his movements "three minutes before it goes off. Everyone's got to get out of the building, now!"

The soldier eyed him suspiciously. "Are you sure?"

"I know what I saw. And from what I'm being told, it's part of a bigger terrorist plot. Everyone needs to get the hell out!"

The officer shook his head, like he was more irritated by the news than anything else, but he lifted his walkie-talkie regardless. "We've got a reported emergency situation. Get everyone in your immediate vicinity to vacate the premises. Do not wait. Get out of the building."

Terre took that as their cue and waved for Annika and Becky to follow him.

"Careful," the soldier said. "There are still live units running around. They shoot first and don't ask questions. I'll be right behind you."

Terre nodded as the three of them ran toward the main exit.

Bodies lay everywhere. Some were still groaning, but most lay quiet, having met their end at the hand of a battlefield robot in a Las Vegas casino.

Soldiers grabbed the innocents closest to them, but there was no way they could bring all the injured out of the hotel in time. It would be impossible to separate the injured from the dead at a moment's notice.

A woman stood beside a craps table, trying to coax her obviously scared children to come out. A male officer tried to convince her they needed to go. Dust coated her panic-stricken face, and her brown hair was waved in an old-fashioned hairdo. Her khaki jacket seemed an odd choice for the eighty-degree heat, though the hotel air conditioning had kept the place quite chilled until the power outage halted its output.

Terre could tell the woman was attempting to coax her kids out from under the table. The officer barked his command at her to leave, which didn't seem to faze her, and moved on, desperate to alert as many able-bodied people as he could have of the impending disaster before he left himself.

Two children sat on the dirtied carpet, dust streaking their faces, incapable of understanding the trauma they had just witnessed: a boy in overalls and a striped shirt, and a girl in a yellow shirt with a flower on it. Both were the spitting image of their mother, with light brown hair and long eyelashes that batted at the surrounding dust.

Terre would not let their uncertainty be their downfall.

"Don't wait for me," he called to Annika and Becky. "Don't stop until you reach the middle of the Strip."

They nodded unquestioningly and picked up their pace.

"Ma'am," Terre said as he approached the woman. "We don't have time to talk them out of this. A bomb's about to go off."

Terre could tell the woman was just as scared as the kids. The trauma in her face told Terre she was frozen with inaction.

Without thinking, he knelt under the table and snatched at the two children, grabbing one under each arm.

"We've got to go now!"

The woman's eyes bulged, outraged that he would dare grab her children, but she could yell at him later. He took off running after Annika and Becky, praying it would enrage the woman enough to follow him and that she wasn't carrying a gun.

His impulsive plan worked. "What the hell do you think you're doing?" she screamed after him, keeping pace with him as he made his way around the remaining slot machines and card tables, avoiding as much death and debris as he could as he pushed his way through the carnage that lay in the main lobby.

"Let us go!" the boy yelled, kicking his legs and pounding his small fists against Terre's back. After everything else Terre had been through, the blows were little more than a moderate irritant, but they were annoying all the same. The girl, who must have been a few years older than her brother, was still in shock, her eyes wide as she absorbed the horrors strewn around them.

The earth shook around him just as Terre reached the lobby door. He didn't stop, and he didn't slow. He didn't look to see if the woman behind him was still following, or if she was joining the others who had been hurtling through the main entrance. The crowd ducked as they ran, afraid the building might collapse on their heads.

The boy stopped his protests as the earth shook, his shouts turning to cries as nearby screams drowned him out. Barks from the military operatives echoed behind them, their shouts of "*Move!*" cutting through the rest of the noise.

"Don't stop!" Terre shouted to nobody in particular as he crossed the threshold. Most didn't listen, but some ran beside him. He prayed the mother of the two children he carried was still on his heels.

His legs propelled him out of the entrance and into the throughway of the hotel, where people were stopping to turn around and look up. Terre didn't have to stop to see the smoke and feel the first specks of debris falling. Terre leaned a shoulder into those standing by. They weren't out of the kill zone, not by a long shot, and he wasn't going to get caught in the crowd.

The earth quaked again, its source seeming further away,

and he cleared the foliage of the property in time to see multiple plumes and bursts of flames lighting the Strip.

The fireballs now erupting from the resorts seemed brighter with the electricity out. The sun was waning in the sky, and the lack of neon lights only highlighted the explosive force. Flames burst from multiple floors of multiple buildings, revealing how highly orchestrated the plan truly was—much more so than he had imagined.

A few bursts and the front of the Venetian resort across the Strip crumbled, screams coming from both behind him and from those who were likely fleeing the resort across the way. Similar lights and bursts of smoke were coming from the Bellagio and the MGM Grand. Nearly every major resort suffered multiple explosions which tore gaping wounds in the boulevard's complexion.

Police bots and their human counterparts were at a standoff. Something had mangled most of their robot dogs, and the rest were running off into the sunset.

This wasn't about military bots and drones any longer; whatever had caused their rebellion against their human masters had spread. Just how far had yet to be seen. Thinking back, there had been destroyed maintenance bots and robot dealers among the deceased within the lobby of the hotel, but whether they had turned on the patrons or were merely collateral damage in the crossfire of Sentinels versus humans, Terre could only speculate.

Annika and Becky waited in the center of the street. As he approached, Terre set the two children down. Other survivors trickled to the center of the boulevard as well, winding their way haphazardly between the abandoned vehicles that still littered the pavement, their mouths agape and their eyes fixed on the buildings deteriorating before them.

The children's mother caught up with them and

embraced the two kids she'd feared were being abducted by a stranger. She couldn't be bothered giving Terre a nod of scorn or even thanks, as her entire focus was covering her children with her own body as best she could, in fear of further fallout from the attack.

The blasts hadn't been enough to bring the buildings down completely—not yet, though the lasting impact on their structural integrity had yet to be seen. There was no telling what the lasting damage would be, but it had been enough of a blast to bring large chunks of the resorts tumbling to the ground, crushing those who had refused to clear enough distance from the property's periphery. Plumes of dirt roiled over the palm trees, parking lots, and sidewalks before billowing out into the street.

Terre covered his nose and mouth, not wanting to inhale too much of what he knew would be toxic material.

He gave Annika a knowing look, and she nodded. An unspoken understanding.

They had to keep moving.

Chapter Twenty-Three

Annika

ANNIKA GRABBED Terre's arm with trepidation and latched onto Becky's hand with her free arm. They would need to avoid being split up among the crowd. Rogue bots and police drones still roamed the streets. Ex-protesters scurried through the smashed windows of shops with goods they had obviously stolen. The dust hadn't even settled, but it was clear Las Vegas would never be the same.

Time seemed to slow as they made their way through the panic-filled streets, the sunlight rapidly fading. The Strip without electricity was an eerie place. The only source of light would soon be the flames flickering within the bombed-out resorts.

Military vehicles worked their way through the side streets as soldiers maneuvered around abandoned rideshares. It seemed to Annika they had quelled some of the robot soldiers—Terre had called them Sentinels—but even if they'd subdued that threat, there would be others they had to deal with: terrorists, looters, and a panicked city without power or a way to communicate with each other.

Screams from people looking for loved ones hauntingly

called above the yells of fear. Families and friends who had been separated between hotels were now desperate to ensure their loved ones hadn't been killed in the bombings, but without a way to connect, most were clearly unsure of where to look and were running headlong toward the last location they were known to be.

Annika felt a pang of jealousy. These people had a thread to pull at; a clue to investigate. Annika had no idea where Ember might have taken Cheyenne—or for what purpose.

The only hope she clung to was that Ember might have done as Terre had suggested and taken her sister to safety. If the bot was still looking out for Cheyenne's best interests, it wouldn't be sitting in the Strip's uncertainty.

Army Humvees rolled onto the Strip now, manually driven and sporting soldiers with megaphones, who directed bystanders to make their way to the nearby stadium and arena.

"A curfew is going into effect," a female soldier declared. "Please check in at one of the two stadiums and await further instructions. If you are stuck in your room or in a casino, help is on the way. If you are already inside a facility and are presently safe, please remain where you are until someone can ensure you have a safe path to exit. Please be patient ..."

Annika stopped paying attention to the message as her feet slapped against the sidewalk. Further down the Strip, she could hear other officers repeating the same message. Gunfire and blaster fire also echoed from somewhere to the north; whether from bots, army, police, or civilians was impossible for her to tell. The standoff between man and machine had slowed, but it clearly wasn't over.

Then Annika saw the orbs.

Terre had mentioned them earlier, but in the chaos, she had put them out of her mind. Blue lights swirled around the black spheres as they hovered in the darkening skies above the city center. Their behemothic size made the fighter jets also circling the city appear like toys.

"Terre?" she said, unsure of what she wanted to ask. They hadn't slowed their pace, so she could barely speak, but she was afraid the worst of what she was to experience that day was yet to come.

"I see them," he replied. Sweat dripped from the man's forehead, but his breathing was even, as though he was barely exerting himself. "Onyx. The military's ultimate fighter drones."

They had run about a mile, passing the MGM Grand, a foreboding mass of emerald architecture in the darkness, before they reached Tropicana Avenue. Terre's first sight of the main highway leading to the airport and out of the city brought a momentary grin to his face.

Annika slowed her pace, sucking in air as her heart rate steadied. Becky caught up beside her, once again gasping for breath, and doubled over, forcing air in and out of her lungs. Considering she had been on the floor not so long ago, it impressed Annika how well her friend was doing, but her friend's well-being wasn't her primary concern.

"I can't leave," Annika said. "Not without Cheyenne."

Terre was several paces ahead of them, turning to round the corner.

They still had to follow the north side of the MGM for another half mile and continue past the airport. Miles of empty vehicles sat on the highway before them. Cheyenne aside, Annika wasn't sure she'd be able to run as far as they'd need to. She hadn't been past the airport before, but she knew there was a long way to go before they were even out of the city. Endless concrete and sand awaited them, and the sun had set. Terre couldn't possibly mean for them to travel at night on foot? Things were bad here on the Strip, but what about the rest of the city? Would the military be patrolling the streets? Would they be forced to register at a FEMA center? Ideas raced around her head in the brief few seconds it took Terre to circle back to her and Becky.

"I can't join you," she said. "I need to find Cheyenne. Ember could have taken her to an evacuation center. I don't know what's waiting for you in the desert, but I do know I probably don't want to be a part of it. I'm sorry."

Terre shook his head and sighed. His gaze went to the orbs still hovering above them. Annika couldn't help but follow his eye.

"You don't have long before they strike," he said. "To be honest, I don't know what they're waiting for."

The roar of an engine prevented Annika from asking the questions on her lips. Headlights approached, seemingly out of place on the otherwise lifeless street. Annika assumed this was the military coming to remind them that a curfew was coming into effect, and that they'd need to head to one of the evacuation centers.

However, instead of an armored Humvee, an antiquated, gas-powered civilian sports utility vehicle pulled up beside them. Outfitted to mimic a military style but without a roof, only minimal bars prevented instant death if the vehicle were to roll over. Inside sat a dark-skinned woman who, in the dark, Annika didn't initially recognize. But familiarity returned as the woman killed the engine and stood, a smirk visible on her face.

Hailey had found them.

Chapter Twenty-Four

Terre

THE LOOK on the Hailey's face was telling. She was proud as punch to have found them and had anticipated that Terre hadn't expected to see her again.

Nothing about the day had gone as planned, and nothing should have surprised him at this point, but seeing Hailey sitting in the convertible, gas-powered SUV gave him hope that something could go right after all, even if it was a minor victory.

Hailey, at least, had survived. Whatever part she had to play in this was apparently not over yet. He couldn't help but admit it relieved him to see her alive and well, not least of which because she could explain to him why she was carrying a military-grade CD-115, and why she had approached him at the bar to begin with.

There was also the question of Annika and her quest to find Cheyenne. While he had no way of keeping Annika from heading back into the city, he knew that trying to find Cheyenne within the evacuation centers would be worse than trying to find a needle in a haystack.

And that was if the teenager was even there, which he highly doubted.

Terre hadn't had time to express the thought to Annika before Hailey's arrival.

"It looks like you have a ride," Annika said, before turning to Becky, who had remained mostly silent since they'd left the hotel. Terre had seen that look before on people who had gone through hell. The woman would deal with a massive dose of PTSD by the time everything was said and done. She was also still dehydrated and suffering from too much sun. A couple of bottles of water and protein bars could only go so far. She needed a good night's rest.

"You don't have to come back if you'd rather press on," Annika said to her friend. "But I can't leave the city knowing she might be back there."

Becky appeared unsure of how to answer. Her eyes flicked longingly from her friend to the Jeep. Terre could read her thoughts; she wanted to be a supportive friend, but a seat in the SUV appeared to be a godsend, regardless of where its destination might be.

"You can't go back," Hailey interrupted. "Those orbs could attack at any moment. You don't want to be in their path."

Annika shook her head, light from the SUV's headlamps bouncing off her face. "You don't understand. My sister wasn't in our room. Her Keeper bot took her somewhere. She might be at one of the evacuation centers. I need to find her."

"She's not back there," Hailey responded, straight-faced and matter-of-fact.

Annika scrunched her face. "What do you mean? Did you see them?"

Terre breathed a sigh of relief. Hailey had echoed the sentiment he hadn't had a chance to express. Of course,

Hailey hadn't seen the missing teenager; she wouldn't have recognized Cheyenne if she tripped over the girl.

"I didn't have to," Hailey said.

Annika's face didn't relax, her arms folding in front of her.

"Your bot will have done one of two things," Hailey continued. "Protect her or harm her. If they weren't in your room, then keeping your sister in a city about to be attacked by Onyx and terrorists isn't a possible course of action. Besides, a bot wouldn't have made it anywhere near the evacuation center, especially one with even a slight resemblance to a Sentinel."

Terre raised an eyebrow. Hailey had left before Annika had revealed any details about Ember. Yet again, the woman's knowledge betrayed she was privy to more information than she had let on.

Hailey was little more than a silhouette standing on her seat in the SUV now, resting her arms on the rollbars above her, but Terre could tell the woman was looking straight at him.

"There are reports that a convoy of bots is rolling through the desert toward the Hoover Dam. Right to where your friend is supposed to be."

"For what purpose?" Terre asked.

"Nobody seems to know. But if Kristopher is a highly capable programmer, I would very much doubt it's a coincidence."

A jet roared overhead, doing a flyby over the Strip. It appeared the military weren't willing to make the first move, instead just maintaining a position in case anything changed.

Not willing to shoot down a multi-million-dollar investment unless absolutely necessary.

Which meant more lives would be lost. At least they had

been willing to send in ground troops to clear the streets. Hopefully it wouldn't end with a massacre from above.

"What does this have to do with Cheyenne?" Annika asked. "Where do you think she is?"

"My guess is, wherever these bots are going, yours is going, too," Hailey replied.

"Why would it take the girl?" Terre asked.

"The same reports are saying there are people within the convoy as well. Pilots have seen the movements during their flybys, but what with everything happening, nobody's been able to spare the manpower to form a strategy."

"And K's involved," Terre thought out loud.

"That's what intel believes," Hailey replied. "That's how Fredricks convinced the powers that be to send you instead of a tactical unit."

Terre's thoughts disappeared as he studied the woman before him. He kicked himself. How could he have been sucked in by a seemingly random meeting at the bar?

"Who are you?" he asked.

"Get in, and I'll explain on the way. Unless you plan on walking, this is the best means of getting there. But I don't have an unlimited amount of gas, and there aren't exactly gas stations along the highway anymore."

Terre rubbed his temple. He didn't want to be involved in this shit, but what were his options? The city was obviously no longer safe, and perhaps he could talk K out of whatever it was he was doing.

It looked like it was up to him to save the world once again.

Terre shook his head and pulled himself into the front passenger seat.

Annika stood where she was, eyeing the city behind them. Shouts from both the National Guard and the police echoed as they ordered people off the streets. Terre could tell she was unsure of her next move.

"I'm with you, whatever you decide," Becky said to Annika. She stared at her friend, waiting for confirmation. "Whatever it takes to find Cheyenne."

"They wouldn't have let your bot near the evacuation centers," Terre said. "And it wouldn't have put itself in a situation where it would have been separated from her."

Annika sighed. "You're right," she said. "I just hate to think she's somewhere alone, scared, and I'm not there with her. She probably has no idea if she'll ever see me again."

Without another word, Annika stepped to the SUV, opened the door behind Terre's seat, and let herself in. Becky followed close behind, getting in on the passenger side.

"All right," Hailey said, starting the vehicle's engine. "We've got people to find. Let's go."

Looking for more?

Artificial Insurrection
Book Three in The Terre Hoffman Chronicles

Order your copy today.

ACKNOWLEDGMENTS

I'd like to thank Pete Smith from Novel Approach Manuscript Services for providing it with multiple edits, and assisting with details and phrasings that I was at a loss for. His efforts have truly brought this work to the next level of refinement.

To Aime Sound at Red Leaf Word Services for the final proofread and catching my Canadian-isms before the book hit the shelves.

The folks at MiblArt have been my cover designers from the beginning, and they outdid themselves with the covers for this series.

And as always to my lovely wife Nettie, who understands my early mornings, late evenings, and weekends at the keyboard. It is truly a blessing to have someone so supportive behind me.

ABOUT THE AUTHOR

Herman Steuernagel is a crafter of dystopian worlds and dark tales, including his debut, internationally bestselling Lies of the Guardians series.

Herman grew up with a love of story and of writing. That love has never waned and led to a Bachelor of Arts (English Major) from the University of Calgary. His past titles include entrepreneur, financial branch manager, and journalist. He currently works as a web developer.

Herman lives in British Columbia, Canada where he wields his stories of robots, vampires and other fantastical creatures. He can often be found cycling, running and enjoying time with his wife.